Addie McCormick

AND THE SECRET OF THE SCARLET BOX

Leanne Lucas

HARVEST HOUSE PUBLISHERS
Eugene, Oregon 97402

**ADDIE McCORMICK AND THE
SECRET OF THE SCARLET BOX**

Copyright © 1994 by Leanne Lucas
Published by Harvest House Publishers
Eugene, Oregon 97402

Library of Congress Cataloging-in-Publication Data

Lucas, Leanne, 1955–
    Addie McCormick and the secret of the scarlet
box / Leanne Lucas.
        p.   cm. — (Addie McCormick adventures ; 7)
    Summary: The discovery of an old metal box
underwater in their favorite creek launches Addie and
Nick on another adventure.
    ISBN 1-56507-230-8
    [1. Mystery and detective stories. 2. Christian life—
Fiction.]
I. Title. II. Series: Lucas, Leanne, 1955– Addie adven-
ture book ; 7.
PZ7.L96963Adcc   1994   94-19369
[Fic]—dc20   CIP
                                                        AC

Printed in the United States of America.

94 95 96 97 98 99 00 — 10 9 8 7 6 5 4 3 2 1

For my mom and dad,
Wayne and Betty Hilst,
With all my love and gratitude,
Pete

About the Author

Leanne Lucas grew up reading mysteries by a creek near her childhood home in central Illinois. Secret visits to a nearby abandoned house later provided the inspiration for many of Addie's adventures. Leanne enjoys naming her characters after friends and family—Addie was named for a woman she worked with at the University of Illinois.

Leanne and her husband, David, own their own business and homeschool their son, Joshua. They reside in Homer, Illinois, where they share their home with Josh's grandma, four hermit crabs, and a cat named Star.

Contents

CHAPTER 1

A Truck and
a Treasure

"Hurry up, Nick!"

Addie's long, black hair whipped across her face as she shouted over her shoulder at her best friend and neighbor, Nick Brady. It was their first trip to the creek since last fall, and Addie was eager to get there. She faced forward on her bike and rode without hands while she pulled her hair back from her face. She wound it tightly and tied it in a thick knot at the nape of her neck. It never stayed that way long, but it would do for now.

She was just finishing the knot when her

ten-speed began to wobble. She grabbed the handle-bars in time to save herself from wiping out in the dusty gravel that edged all the country roads in Mason County. She glanced over her shoulder, pre-pared to face Nick's teasing grin, but Nick was nowhere in sight.

"Where did he disappear to?" she mumbled into the wind that blew her bangs off her forehead. "He was right behind me!"

About fifty yards down the road, she saw Nick's bike on its side, the front wheel still spinning. Nick was sitting at the bottom of a shallow ditch. He had pulled the tail of his oversized tee shirt down to mop up the blood that was pouring out of the gash in his knee, which Addie could see through the huge rip in his new blue jeans.

"Nick, your mom is going to—"

"Don't say it!" Nick interrupted her.

"She told you to change your clothes before we—"

"I said, don't say it!" he growled. "Besides, this is your fault."

"*My* fault?"

"I was trying to catch up with you! 'Hurry up, Nick. Hurry up, Nick.'" He imitated Addie in a whiny singsong voice. "Why didn't you wait for me like I asked?"

"I waited for you for fifteen minutes. If I hadn't left, you'd still be home fooling around with that stupid chain."

"That 'stupid chain' slipped off again! That's why I fell. If you'd given me time to fix it before we left, this never would have happened."

Addie frowned, unable to come up with a suitable retort. Finally she muttered, "Why don't you get a new bike? That one's falling apart."

Nick just frowned at her and continued dabbing at the blood on his knee. They both knew he didn't need a new bike.

Addie dropped her ten-speed to the ground and joined Nick in the ditch. She squatted next to him and peered at his wound, wrinkling her nose at the gruesome sight. It was quite a cut, with bits of gravel ground into his knee and fresh blood mixing with blood that had already dried to a dark red.

When she reached out to brush some of the gravel off his leg, Nick smacked her hand. "Don't touch it," he snapped.

"Well, excuse me." Addie clambered back up the ditch and picked up her bicycle. "It's not that bad. You'll live. Let's go."

Nick winced as he stood up. He looked at his blood-soaked tee shirt and sighed. "Does blood come out or is this ruined too?"

"My mom says if you get a blood stain in cold water right away, most of it will come out."

Nick's expression brightened. "The water at the creek is pretty cold."

"Your mom told you not to get wet."

Nick gave Addie a disgusted stare and gestured at his ripped jeans and bloody shirt. "Like that's going to make a difference now."

Addie finally grinned. "You're probably right. What is it Miss T. says? 'In for a dime, in for a dollar.'" Miss T. was their elderly neighbor and a good friend to both the children. Her conversations were always sprinkled with old-fashioned expressions that made a lot of sense, once you figured them out.

Nick shook his head. "What's that mean, anyway? I don't understand what she's saying half the time." He picked up his ten-speed and fitted the chain back on the sprocket.

Addie laughed. "I think in this case, it means getting wet is probably going to be the least of your problems!"

Nick mounted his bike and began pedaling, but stopped quickly when his jeans rubbed against the injured knee. "Ooooooowwwwwwww!"

"You take pain so well, Nick," Addie said. "Did that help?"

Nick gave his friend a sheepish grin. "Not really. Just ride slowly, okay?" Even though the day was fairly cool, his dark blond hair was curling damply, and he wiped a band of sweat from his forehead. Addie felt sorry for him.

"Okay," she said.

With the wind at their back, Nick was able to coast most of the way to the creek, one of their favorite hideouts and places to play. Addie dropped her bike in the weeds at the side of the road and ran lightly to the edge of the steep embankment, with Nick hobbling behind her. She stopped short in dismay at the sight she saw.

The stream that once flowed freely through the fields was now still. Patches of moss and algae covered much of the stagnant water, and dead branches, brown and slimy, bobbed silently against one another. The narrow strip of sandy beach, where they usually left their shoes when they went wading, had disappeared under water. Although the wildflowers that came with spring were beginning to appear on both sides of the ditch, most of the young trees near the water's edge were stripped of their branches or laid flat. Nick sank to the ground, his knee forgotten, and Addie joined him.

Finally Nick spoke. "Did the tornado do this?"

Addie nodded. "It must have."

Six weeks earlier a tornado had swept through Mason County. The town of Mt. Pilot had been hit the hardest, losing its grade school, several homes, and untold roofs and small out-buildings.

"I didn't even think about something like this happening," Nick said in a quiet voice.

Addie was silent, saddened by the dismal sight. When she moved to Illinois, almost a year ago, this creek had been one of her first discoveries. Losing it was like losing a friend.

"Do you think we could clean it up?" Nick asked her.

She wrinkled her nose. "I'm not wading into that mess! Are you?"

Nick frowned. "Well, not with that slimy stuff floating on top. But there's got to be something blocking it downstream. That's why it's stopped flowing. If we clear away whatever's blocking it, it would clean itself up, right?"

Addie looked doubtful. "Whatever's blocking it must be pretty big. I don't think we could move it."

"How will we know unless we try?" Nick persisted. "Come on, let's go look."

He half-ran, half-skipped back to the road, favoring his knee. Addie followed him to the embankment on the other side, and together they peered down the ditch, but there was no sign of any blockage. The water there was blanketed with moss and algae, and they could hear the hum of a cloud of mosquitoes across the stream.

"It must be down farther," Nick said. "But we're getting closer. You can tell by all the brush and branches clogging up the water. Let's keep going."

They struck out into the field, walking along the top of the embankment. They hadn't walked far before the stream grew very narrow and curved gently to the south. Nick let out a shout of excitement and Addie gasped. There, on its side and wedged tightly between the steep banks of the little creek, was a very old, very dirty, Chevy pickup truck.

The children stared, first at the truck, then at one another. Without a word, they both scrambled down the steep slope. Addie stopped before she reached the water's edge, but Nick waded in ankle-deep, balancing himself on the front bumper of the old truck.

"Where do you suppose this came from?" he asked.

Addie thought carefully, then pointed to the south. "Remember that deserted farmhouse just down the road? It was demolished in the tornado. Dad said the old shed that went with it was full of junk cars and trucks. The tornado scattered them all through Ron Kleiss's cornfield. I bet this truck came from that shed."

Nick took a deep breath. "That's about an eighth of a mile away. Scary, isn't it?"

Addie nodded. "I don't ever want to see another tornado as long as I live." She shivered. The memory of that day was very vivid. If she dwelled on those memories, she could still hear the roar of the tornado, a sound unlike anything she'd ever heard before. So she didn't dwell on it.

Be anxious for nothing, but in everything by prayer and supplication, let your requests be made known unto God. And the peace of God, which passes all understanding, shall keep your hearts and minds in Christ Jesus. The verse came easily to her, and the fears of that day slipped away.

"Ron had all the other vehicles towed. I wonder why he didn't have this one pulled out?" Addie mused.

"He probably doesn't know it's here," Nick told her. "It's been raining off and on for the last six weeks. Most farmers haven't been in the fields since early April."

Addie nodded. "Ron told my dad crops were going to be real late this year. He said . . . Nick, what are you doing?"

Nick had waded a few steps further into the stagnant water. He was reaching under the truck, trying to clear away some of the brush that had wedged itself between the bottom of the pickup and the streambed.

"If we could just clear this mess out under here," Nick grunted, "we could get the water flowing again."

"Be careful!" Addie admonished him. "What if you pull something loose and the whole truck falls over on you?"

"Who are you, my mother?" Nick muttered. He yanked hard at a long, shriveled limb, and it came out easily, throwing him off-balance. He stepped back with his right foot to catch himself. But his left leg caught on something underwater, and he toppled over backwards onto the bank. He landed with a hard thump, then flopped onto his back and groaned.

"What, are you hurt?" Addie asked.

"No," he sighed, "but I just ripped my other pant leg."

Addie choked back a laugh and watched as Nick sat up and reluctantly reached into the slimy water and tugged at the hem of his jeans until he was free. Then he frowned and stuck his hand back into the water a second time.

"I don't know what I was caught on, but it wasn't the truck," he said with a frown. He fished around in the muck for several long moments.

Addie just closed her eyes and sighed. She knew it wouldn't do any good to warn Nick about the dangers of rusty metal or broken glass, or the infections he could get from that yucky water.

"What *is* this?" Nick said softly. He had both hands in the water now, trying to dislodge his discovery. "Come here and help me."

"No way!"

"Sometimes Addie..." Nick said between puffs of breath, "you...are such a...*girl!*"

With that insult, he pulled his treasure free. He almost fell again, but he caught himself this time and hauled a metal box to the edge of the water and onto the bank.

Addie crouched beside him and Nick grinned. "Oh, now you want to help, huh?"

Addie ignored him. "What is it?"

He shrugged. "Some kind of box. Let's see if we can...uh, oh."

"What's the matter?"

Nick pointed silently to a message scratched crudely in the metal.

DO NOT OPEN UNDER PENALTY OF LAW

CHAPTER 2

The Danner Brothers

"That's not legal or anything, is it?" Nick asked.

"Of course it is!" Addie sputtered.

"It's just scratched on with a nail," Nick said.

"Because the owner doesn't want you or me or anyone else opening that box," Addie told him.

Nick still tried to pry open the lid, but it was locked. "Look how old this is, Addie," he said. "The owner probably forgot he ever had it."

The box did look old. There were two rusty screws where a handle had once been, and all the corners were pockmarked with rust.

"Let's take it home and show my dad," Addie suggested.

"Are you going to carry it?"

"Oh." Addie wrinkled her nose. "I guess that won't work, will it? We'll get my dad to bring us back in the car. He'll be just as interested in it as we are."

Nick agreed, and together they walked back to the main road. Nick's shoes squished noisily. They picked up their bikes and headed for home. The sun was still shining, and the wind had died down.

Mr. McCormick's car was in the driveway when the two children rounded the corner to Addie's house. Her father was sitting on the edge of the porch, drinking ice tea and watching her mother plant impatiens in the front flower bed. Addie stood up to pedal into the yard. Nick followed slowly behind her.

"Dad! Mom!" Addie was shouting even though her parents were just a few feet away. "You'll never guess what we found at the creek!"

Mr. McCormick smiled at his excited daughter. "Dinosaur bones."

"Oh, Dad—" Addie began.

But Mr. McCormick's smile faded. He set his tea on the porch and jumped to the ground. "Nick, what happened? Are you all right?"

Mrs. McCormick looked up from her flowers and drew in a sharp breath. "Oh, Nick!"

Addie frowned. What was the big deal? Then she took her first good look at Nick since they'd left home an hour earlier.

His once-white tee shirt was now almost covered with a combination of mud and blood. The hem on one leg of his blue jeans was ripped and hanging. The tear in the knee on his other leg had widened, and his cut was bleeding again. His shoes were muddy, his jeans were wet, and his hands, arms, and face were covered with scum-colored water spots.

Nick grinned cheerfully. "I'm fine," he said. "I just look half-dead."

"But your knee is bleeding badly," Mrs. McCormick said.

"It does hurt a little," Nick admitted. "The chain on my bike slipped and this," he gestured to his knee, "is what happened."

"Ouch," Mr. McCormick said, and Mrs. McCormick winced.

"How did you get so wet?" she asked.

"That's what I was trying to tell you," Addie interrupted. "We found an old Chevy truck damming up the creek!"

"In the drainage ditch?" Mr. McCormick was incredulous.

Addie nodded. "I think the twister flipped it through the field from that old shed," she explained. "The creek is dammed up and everything's getting slimy and it smells gross."

Nick sniffed the sleeve of his tee shirt. "Like this," he said helpfully and held out his arm.

Mr. McCormick backed away and shook his head. "I'd rather see for myself," he said and grinned at his wife. "Want to come along?"

"Sure," she said. She gazed at Nick. "We really should drop you off at home. I hate to see you ride that bike if the chain needs work and—"

"Can I go with you to the creek first?" Nick pleaded. "I want to be there when you open the box."

"What box?" Mr. McCormick asked.

"We found a big metal box, but it's locked," Addie said.

"Does it have a name on it?"

Addie shook her head. "I didn't see one."

"We didn't really look for a name," Nick reminded her. "We saw that warning on the top, so we didn't look any farther."

"*What* warning?" Mrs. McCormick asked.

"Something about being under the 'penalty of the law,'" Nick said in a dramatic voice.

"Let's take a look at this box," Mr. McCormick said.

Mrs. McCormick found an old towel for Nick to sit on in the car, and Addie's father sped down the country road to the creek. Addie and Nick led her parents through the field, and the children and Mr. McCormick slid down the embankment to the battered truck. Mrs. McCormick held back.

"John, that's going to ruin your shoes. Addie, don't get those good pants wet. I said . . . Oh, for heaven's sake," she muttered and picked her way through the weeds down to the water's edge.

"Ron will have to hook onto this with his tractor and pull it out," Mr. McCormick told his wife, "or his field won't drain properly, and he'll lose money."

He knelt beside the rusty metal box at the water's edge. "'Do not open under penalty of law,'" he read. "Okay, we won't. Nick, help me haul this up to the road."

Mrs. McCormick spread out some old newspapers in the back of the station wagon, and Mr. McCormick hoisted the box into the car.

"Can we open it when we get home, Dad?" Addie asked.

Her father hesitated. "I'd rather not, but we might not have any choice. It could be the only way to find the owner."

"Let's ask Miss T.," Addie's mother said.

"Why her?" Nick wanted to know.

"She lives right up the road. She might know who owns the house, or at least who lived there before it was abandoned."

"Good idea," Mr. McCormick told his wife.

Everyone climbed back in the car, and Mr. McCormick drove to "the mansion," as Addie and Nick liked to call the graceful Victorian home. Miss T. was a spinster in her late seventies who'd recently acquired a great deal of money. She spent much of it remodeling her home, inside and out.

When they pulled into the driveway, Addie could see Miss T. and her friend Amy on their hands and knees in the flower bed, planting bulbs of some kind. Amy Takahashi lived as a companion with Miss T. and did many of the things Miss T. was no longer able to do.

Mr. McCormick eased the car down the long drive and stopped near the back door. Amy waved and Miss T. struggled to her feet. Addie could see the older woman instructing Amy on where to plant the rest of the bulbs. Then she walked slowly over to their car.

"This is a surprise," Miss T. said bluntly.

Addie and Nick both grinned. When they first met Miss T., they were a little frightened of her. But they soon discovered her gruff exterior covered a very kind heart and a good sense of humor.

"We've got something to show you," Addie said. She and Nick ran to the back of the car and opened the back door. Addie's parents followed more slowly, talking with the older woman.

"Addie and Nick found an old metal box down in the creek," Mr. McCormick told her. "We thought you might be able to help us figure out who it belongs to."

Mr. McCormick told Miss T. about the pickup truck and their suspicions that the box was from the same property. Miss T. listened, all the while giving the metal box a thorough examination. She traced over the scratched letters on the top with a careful finger, then turned the box on end and scanned the bottom as well.

Mr. McCormick finished his explanation, and Miss T. found what she was looking for. In the right-hand bottom corner were the initials SMD.

The old woman drummed her fingers on the rusty metal. "I used to know the name of those people. Can't think of it now, though. It'll come to me. Why don't you bring that box inside, and I'll tell you what I do remember. There was quite a tragedy there, years and years ago."

Addie and Nick exchanged excited glances. They all went inside, and Miss T. fixed coffee and sodas for her visitors while she told them her story.

"First of all," the old woman began, "you have to remember I had just moved here myself when this tragedy took place. I didn't know a soul, but my sister did and she kept me up on the latest gossip. I'm telling you that because I want you to know this whole story might be true. Then again, it might not."

Nick grinned. "I think that's why they call it gossip."

Miss T. ignored him. "Two brothers lived in that house fifty years ago. They were young men, barely out of high school. Both their parents were dead, so they lived there together and farmed the land. What *was* their name? Anyway, I saw them myself several times. Different as night and day. But they were inseparable. Until the war. The war changed everything."

"What war was that?" Nick asked.

"What a question!" Miss T. exclaimed. "What war do you *think* was going on fifty years ago, young man?"

Addie was standing behind Miss T. and she waved two fingers at Nick over the old woman's shoulder.

"World War II, of course," Nick answered promptly.

Miss T. gave Addie a suspicious glance, then turned back to Nick. "Of course," was all she said and continued her story.

"The Japanese bombed Pearl Harbor in '41 and America joined the war. One of the brothers got called up, and the other one didn't. It caused quite a division between them."

"Called up?" Addie asked.

"Drafted," Miss T. explained. "I don't think I ever knew why one brother didn't have to go to war, but he didn't."

Nick was puzzled. "Why would they fight about who got to go to war?"

"Back then, most men were willing to serve their country by going to war," Miss T. explained. "But some men saw it as more than a duty. It was an honor, an accomplishment. That's how the second brother saw it. The one who *didn't* get drafted."

"So he was jealous of the brother who did go to war," Addie said.

Miss T. nodded. "Exactly. Especially when the brother who *did* get drafted didn't really believe in war."

"What a stupid thing to fight about," Nick said. "Why didn't they just trade places?"

Mr. McCormick grinned. "The government tends to frown on that kind of behavior, Nick."

"Anyway," Miss T. continued, "while brother number one was in basic training, brother number two married his sweetheart."

Addie gasped. "You mean the second brother married the first brother's girlfriend?"

Miss T. nodded. "Brother number one came home on furlough, took all his belongings, and left—for good. About six months later brother number two grew very ill. He died within the year."

"Did brother number one come back and marry the widow?" Addie asked.

Miss T. shook her head. "He was declared missing in action soon after he was shipped overseas. I don't know the end of his story."

"What happened to the widow?" Nick wanted to know.

"She was pregnant when her husband died. She gave birth to the baby but died from complications." Then Miss T. snapped her fingers. "Danner. Her name was Stella Danner. Frank and Sidney were the brothers."

CHAPTER 3

The Scarlet Box

"How sad," Mrs. McCormick murmured. Addie nodded in agreement.

Nick was practical. "If they're all dead, can we open the box?"

Everyone stared at him.

"Hey, I'm as sad as the rest of you," he said. "If we have a moment of silence, *then* can we open the box?"

Addie made a face at him, but Mr. McCormick rose to his feet. "In memory of all the Danners, dead and gone," he said in a solemn tone. Then he turned to Miss T. "Got a crowbar?"

Even Addie laughed at that, and Miss T. stepped out on her back porch. She returned to the kitchen with a flat bar in her hand. "A crowbar won't work," she said. "Too thick. Try this. And put that box in the sink. There might be water in it. I don't want it all over my kitchen floor."

Mr. McCormick carried the box to the sink, and Addie and Nick crowded around him. He slipped one end of the flat bar under the lip of the box and popped it open with one quick motion. Water dripped off the top.

"Is everything ruined?" Addie asked.

Mr. McCormick shook his head. "No. Whoever packed this wanted it to last," he said. "Everything is wrapped in oilskin."

Miss T. wiped up the water dripping down the front of her cabinet while Mr. McCormick lifted a large bag out of the box. Water beaded on the outside, but it was obvious none had gotten inside. Every seam was sewn tight. It looked like a hard, lumpy pillow. Miss T. patted it dry with her towel.

Then she pulled a pair of heavy-duty scissors out of a cabinet drawer and handed them to Mr. McCormick. He cut off one end of the bag with a few short snips. Then he slid the contents of the bag onto the countertop.

Addie gave a squeal of delight, and Nick let out a whoop. "Cool!" he said. He reached out and picked up a small, roughly carved wooden horse. Addie chose a yo-yo, and Mrs. McCormick reached for a top. That left Addie's father several oddly shaped pieces of wood which he quickly fit together to make a puzzle of a dog.

The only thing left was a small leather bag. Miss T. picked it up and tried to pull open the drawstring, but it was too tight for her arthritic fingers. She handed it to Addie.

The young girl managed to get one finger inside the bag and pulled gently until the leather loosened up. Then she reached inside and brought out a beautiful scarlet box. The box fit easily in the palm of her hand. A magnificent soldier was hand-painted on the top. She set it gently on the kitchen table and everyone was silent. Finally, Mrs. McCormick spoke.

"That's . . . not a toy," she said.

Miss T. shook her head. "No, it's not. It's an antique."

"But why was it with all these toys?" Nick wanted to know. "Somebody carved these other things, probably a kid. Why would you put an antique with a bunch of kid stuff?"

"There's something inside," Addie said. "I could feel it rolling around. Maybe it is a toy of some kind. A rich kid's toy."

Mr. McCormick picked up the box and tugged on the lid. The box was well made and the lid fit snugly, but it came off with little problem. Inside were four very old marbles and two small slips of paper.

"Cat's eyes," Miss T. said as she examined one of the marbles. "You don't see many of these anymore."

"What do those papers say?" Addie's fingers fairly itched to snatch one from her father's hand, but she restrained herself. "What do they say?"

Mr. McCormick gave his daughter one while he opened the other. Nick looked over her shoulder as Addie read out loud.

> *Dear Frankie,*
> *Remember these toys? Mama saved them. I'm sorry I can't be there to go on the scavenger hunt with you this time.*
> *Have enough fun for both of us. Sid*

"What scavenger hunt?" Nick wanted to know.

Mr. McCormick grinned and waved the small paper he held. "Listen to this."

> *Here it begins, and here it ends,*
> *Always brothers, sometimes friends.*
> *Though this scarlet box divides us still,*
> *Follow the clues and believe what you will.*
>
> *Smelly, dark, beneath the ground,*
> *Where the carrots and spuds are found.*
> *There you'll find the first of four,*
> *Just inside the open door.*

Miss T. laughed. "Sidney must have hidden something in a root cellar."

"What's a root cellar?" Nick asked.

"An underground room where people stored vegetables so they wouldn't spoil," the older woman explained.

"Do you suppose the cellar is still there?" Addie asked.

"Still *where?*" Nick said.

"On the Danner property," she replied. "If this came from the Danners' house, then Frankie must be the brother who went to war. Sidney was the brother who died. That's why he couldn't be there to go on the scavenger hunt again."

"What do you mean, again?" asked Nick.

"Don't you see? They must have gone on a scavenger hunt together when they were young. Sidney set up another hunt for Frankie. But Frankie never came home from the war, and Sidney died too. That's why this stuff is still here. We've got the first clue to a fifty-year-old scavenger hunt!"

The three adults had been listening to the exchange, and Addie's mother finally interrupted. "Addie, I'm not going to let you go snooping around the Danner property."

"Why not?" her daughter protested.

"Because anything underground fifty years ago is probably a dangerous place today."

Addie sighed and looked at her father. He grinned.

"Don't take her side," Mrs. McCormick warned.

"I'm not taking sides," Mr. McCormick laughed. "But she might be right. Maybe we could poke around there tomorrow. I'll go with them and make sure they don't get into any trouble."

"It's trespassing."

"Ron Kleiss rents it. I'll check with him first."

"Oh, all right," Mrs. McCormick said. "Just be careful."

Both children grinned, and Mr. McCormick gave

his wife a loud smacking kiss on her cheek. "We will, Mama. You can trust me."

"*You're* the one I'm most worried about."

* * *

The next morning, Addie's father rattled her doorknob before eight. "Rise and shine, kiddo," he called through the closed door. "I've got a meeting down at the station at ten o'clock. If you want to go to the Danners', we have to do it now."

"I'm awake," Addie yelled. She flung back her covers and hopped out of bed. Five minutes later she was dressed and at the kitchen table.

Mrs. McCormick was flipping pancakes at the stove. "How many, Addie?"

Addie hesitated. Usually she could eat five or six of her mom's special pancakes, but today she was in a hurry. "Just three," she said relucantly.

The phone rang and Addie answered it. It was Nick. "When are we going to the Danners'?" he asked.

"In about fifteen minutes," Addie told him. "Dad has to be in Mt. Pilot at ten."

"I'll be right there," Nick said and hung up without saying goodbye.

He was at the back door in a matter of minutes. Of course, he had to have some of Mrs. McCormick's pancakes, so it was past eight-thirty before they were ready to leave.

"Why don't you two ride your bikes?" Mr. McCormick suggested.

"Good idea," Addie said and gulped down the rest of her orange juice. "We'll leave now. You can follow us in about five minutes. That way you can have one more cup of coffee, right?"

Her father just grinned.

It was a cool spring morning, but the sun was warm, and Addie could tell she would be hot in her jeans and sweatshirt later in the day. She and Nick flew down the country road, past Miss T.'s house. Miss T. and Amy were already in the yard, planting more bulbs. Amy waved at the two children, but Miss T. didn't notice them.

"Do you think Miss T. is . . . slowing down a little?" Nick asked.

Addie sighed. "A little." It was hard to watch people you love grow old. "I think she needs a new hearing aid."

Nick sniffed. "I don't know about that. She sure hears what she wants to hear."

Addie chuckled to herself. They'd been caught more than once whispering behind their elderly friend's back—usually when they were planning something they shouldn't be.

The Danner property was just ahead, and Addie forgot about Miss T. She and Nick pulled in the drive and skidded to a stop next to the crumbled foundation of the demolished house.

Someone had cleaned up the yard, but there was still a jumbled mess of bricks, plaster, and old lumber where the house had collapsed on itself during the tornado. The basement was exposed in several places, and Addie knew it would be foolish to risk going down there.

She heard her father's car pull in the drive, and she waved at him. He turned off the motor and joined the children as they circled the perimeter of the old house.

"Well, let's look around, shall we?" Mr. McCormick said. There was a large barn south of the house. Parts of its north and east walls had gaping holes in them. The shed where all the vehicles had been stored was no longer there. Only the foundation, part of the south wall, and a dirt floor remained. "A root cellar could be anywhere. Let's look in that barn first," he said.

They crossed the yard, and Nick peered cautiously around the wooden barn door that was hanging open on one hinge. Mr. McCormick went in first and walked around. Considering the beating it had taken, the barn was still remarkably sturdy. He motioned the children inside.

They all searched the building carefully for any underground storage compartment or room, but they were disappointed. They finally gave up, but not before Nick found an old ladder propped on the south wall. It led to the hayloft.

The young boy looked at Mr. McCormick hopefully. "What do you think?" he asked.

Mr. McCormick laughed. "Not on your life," he said. At the look of disappointment on both children's faces, he relented. "At least, not today. Maybe we'll come back some day when I have more time. Every kid should get the chance to crawl around in a hayloft once in their life."

The three of them went back outside into the bright sunshine. Addie spoke first. "Well, thanks anyway, Dad. I guess we were—"

"You're not giving up, are you?" Mr. McCormick interrupted his daughter with a smile. "Come on."

He strode briskly through the overgrown yard, out toward the field. Addie and Nick hurried after him.

"Sometimes people put their storm cellars, or root cellars, near their gardens." He was walking slowly now, stomping down the dead brush and weeds that reached above his knees. "The entrance was above ground, built at an angle, about thirty degrees. Like this!" he said triumphantly.

He kicked gently at one particularly tall patch of dead grass, and Addie heard a muffled thump. They all dropped to their knees and began pulling up the dry weeds. Hidden under the tangled mass of dried-up vines and brush was a weathered, wooden door. It was locked, but when Mr. McCormick pulled on the rusty handle, it came off in his hand, lock and all. He got his fingers under the door and pulled it open. The wood creaked in protest, and a hinge broke. Mr. McCormick eased the door back on its remaining hinge and rested it on the ground.

Addie and Nick peered into the inky hole. It smelled old and musty, and the air was cold. There were several wooden steps leading into the blackness. Mr. McCormick pulled a small flashlight out of his front shirt pocket. He grinned at the surprised look on the two children's faces.

"Always be prepared," he said. "Wait here. I'll check this out."

He descended the steps, and Addie could see him stoop over before he went through the entrance at the bottom. Several long seconds passed, then he reappeared at the door. "Come on down," he said. "Watch your heads."

Addie went first, and Nick was right on her heels. Her head brushed the top of the doorway and her nose wrinkled at the heavy, earthy smell. Her father was standing, bent over awkwardly in the middle of a very small, square room. It was no more than six feet long, six feet wide and six feet high. The walls were bricked all around, the ceiling was wooden, and the floor was dirt.

The beam of the flashlight shone on their faces, and the three of them stared at one another. Addie began to laugh.

"We sure can't do anything with three of us in here," she said. "There's hardly room to turn around."

Mr. McCormick agreed. "I have to leave, anyway. There's no way you can hurt yourselves down here. This root cellar was built to last. Look around if you want to, and be sure and shut the door when you leave, okay?"

He gave Nick the small flashlight and pulled a larger one out of his back pocket. He handed that one to Addie. "Promise me you won't go near the house or in the barn again," he said.

"I promise," Addie said. "We'll go right home." She paused. "Thanks, Dad."

"No problem, kiddo," he said and kissed his daughter on the forehead. "Have fun."

After her father left, there was a little more room to move around, but not much reason to. There was absolutely nothing in the cellar. As their eyes became accustomed to the light from the steps, Addie switched off her flashlight.

Nick stood in the middle of the room. "This is kind of stupid," he said. "There's nothing here."

"The clue said we would find the 'first of four, just inside the open door.'"

"First of four what?" Nick muttered. "We don't even know what we're looking for."

"Oh, come on, Nick," Addie said. "How should I know? I just thought it would be fun to see if—" She stopped and frowned.

"What is it?" Nick asked her.

She studied the bricks on one side of the door and then pointed to the bricks on the opposite side. "Look at the—what do you call it?—the mortar in between these bricks. See how dark it is? But the mortar over here is lighter. At least it's lighter right here."

Addie reached up to touch the wall, and the bricks moved under her fingers, making a scratching sound. She flicked her flashlight back on. Nick shut his off and tossed it to the ground. Then he dug his pocketknife out of his jeans. He slipped the blade under one of the loose bricks, and it came out easily. They pulled three more out in quick succession.

Nick reached into the hole they had made, and

his yell echoed loudly in the small room. He pulled out a small bag, and Addie shone her flashlight on it. It was made of oilskin and the seams were sewn tightly.

CHAPTER 4

The Wooden Man

Addie could hardly believe their good fortune. "Oh, thank You, thank You, thank You!"

Nick stared at her and shrugged. "You're welcome."

"I was talking to God," she said and thumped the back of Nick's head with her finger.

"Ouch!" He ducked away from her and held the bag at arm's length when she tried to pull it out of his hand. "Don't get grabby!" he said.

"Nick!" she yelled and ran after him as he ducked through the door and raced up the steps into the bright sunshine.

Once outside, they both pulled on the seams of the bag, but it was pointless. This package had been sewn as tightly as the first one.

"We'll have to cut it open," Addie told him. "Let's go back to my house."

"No." Nick shook his head. "Miss T. has scissors we can use, and her house is closer."

"But I want my mom to see this," Addie argued.

"She can see it later. I want to see it now," Nick retorted. He still clutched the bag in one hand. "We don't always have to do things your way. You're not in charge."

"We wouldn't even be here if it weren't for me," Addie said sharply. "I was the one who thought of this."

"And I went along with you. I agreed to do what you wanted to do. Now you should do what *I* want to do."

Addie bit her lip to keep from saying something mean. She turned around and headed down the steps. "I'm going to put those bricks back."

She took her time and finally Nick shouted, "I'm leaving! Are you coming or not?"

Addie walked back up the steps. The door was laying open on the ground, and she reached down to pull it up and back over the opening. Nick just watched her. It took all her strength, but she finally managed to get behind it, and the door fell with a slam. "Let's go," she said.

Neither of them spoke on the bike ride to Miss T.'s house. Addie followed Nick silently down the drive to the backyard. Miss T. and Amy were still up to their elbows in dirt.

Nick dropped his bike to the ground and hurried over to his elderly friend. "May we use your scissors again, Miss T.?"

Miss T. looked over the top of her sunglasses at the package Nick held in his hands. "What have you got there?"

"We found that root cellar on the Danner property. This package was hidden in the wall behind some bricks." Nick paused. "Addie was right. It is a fifty-year-old scavenger hunt." He glanced back at Addie, but she refused to meet his eyes.

Amy smiled. "Eunice has told me of your metal box and the toys inside. I hope to see them. What do you suppose is in this package?"

"Why don't we find out?" Miss T. said briskly. "Scissors are in the kitchen." She got to her feet and brushed her hands on the front of her Bermuda shorts. There were two big dirt spots right above her knees.

Nick ran ahead and let himself in the back door. Miss T. and Amy hurried after him, but Addie lagged behind. At the top of the steps, Miss T. turned and motioned to the young girl.

"Well, come on, miss, or he'll be opening that package without you."

Addie picked up her pace just a fraction. She trudged up the porch steps, and Miss T. laid a gentle hand on her shoulder.

"What's the problem?" she asked.

Addie just shrugged and shook her head. "Nothing, really," she said. She pushed past Miss T. into the kitchen.

Nick was standing by the counter, scissors in hand. "About time," he muttered. "May I open the package now?" he asked with exaggerated politeness. When Addie didn't answer, he snipped into the material carelessly.

"Careful!" Miss T. admonished him and thumped him on the back of the head with her finger. Nick ducked to one side and frowned at the elderly woman.

Addie hid a smile behind her hand, but Nick caught it and shot her a dark look. She choked back a giggle and Nick finally grinned.

"You two sure enjoy giving me grief, don't you?" he mumbled.

"Behave yourself and maybe we wouldn't," Miss T. said tartly. "Whatever you've got there isn't yours and it could be very . . . valuable." Her voice trailed off.

Nick held a small wooden figure in the palm of his hand. The body was flat, square at the shoulders, with two holes where arms should be. Small bits of rock had been tapped into the wood to serve as buttons. At the waist, the wood tapered in on both sides to indicate legs. The head was a small round knob with two rock eyes and a crooked smile scratched into the wood.

"Real valuable," Nick said. "Why's he got that stub coming out of the top of his head?"

"He's missing a part," Addie said. "Probably a hat."

"His arms are gone, too," Nick said. He held the figure up to his eye and squinted through the arm hole that went all the way through the body. "Yep, this here is a real valuable work of art," he drawled.

"Oh, hush," Miss T. said good-naturedly. "Look how worn he is. It's obvious he was played with a lot. He was valuable to somebody."

"Maybe his hat and arms are inside the bag," Amy suggested.

Addie snatched the bag off the counter before Nick could get to it. She searched the inside, but there were no more body parts to be found. Only a scrap of paper.

The writing on this clue was not as legible as the first, and Addie held it up to the window, squinting, trying to read the faded words.

> The second of four is a sure bet.
> Take off your shoes, or they'll get wet.
> Look under the span where horses trot,
> And careful searching will find the slot.

"What does that mean?" Nick grumbled. "Sidney Danner sure won't win any awards for his poetry."

"Hush," Addie said. "We're looking for some place with water, because we have to take our shoes off..."

"How do you look under a span?" Nick wanted to know. "What *is* a span?"

"A span is something... something that hooks things..." Miss T. struggled for the right words. "...Something that connects one part... one side ... to another."

"Like a bridge?" Nick offered.

Miss T. nodded. "Exactly."

"A bridge? A bridge!" Addie slapped Nick on the back. "That's it, Nick. The next," she gestured toward the little wooden figure, "thing is hidden under a bridge. We have to take our shoes off, horses trot over it. It's a bridge!"

"But where's the bridge?" Nick's question dampened Addie's enthusiasm.

"It has to be somewhere near the Danner house," she said.

"Do bridges last fifty years?" he asked.

"I don't know," she said. "But it won't hurt to look, right?"

"Yeah," Nick agreed, "I guess you're right." He studied the wooden figure in his hand. "What are we going to do with four of these ugly little guys?"

Addie laughed. "I don't know. We'll worry about that after we've found them all. Come on, let's go show this to my mom." She slipped the clue back in the bag, and Nick dropped the figure in as well. They thanked Miss T. and Amy for their help and ran out the back door.

The two children rode silently down the road to Addie's house, but this time their silence was a comfortable one. Finally Addie spoke.

"Nick, do you really think I want to be in charge all the time?" she asked.

Nick hesitated and glanced at his friend out of the corner of his eye before he answered. "Well, don't you?"

"No!" Addie protested.

"But you always act like you know exactly what you're doing and why you're doing it and how it should be done," Nick said. "I feel kind of stupid next to you."

"You're the one who figured out the second clue," Addie reminded him.

Nick shook his head. "I figured out span was another word for bridge. You're the one who made the connection with the clue."

"I couldn't have made the connection if you hadn't figured out the definition," Addie argued back.

Nick began to laugh. "Are we fighting about why we were fighting?"

"No."

"Yes, we are."

"No, we're not!"

They stared at one another and burst into laughter.

"Okay," Addie said, "whatever it is we're arguing about, let's stop. And if I get too bossy, just tell me, okay?"

"Okay," Nick agreed.

"I mean it, Nick. Don't worry about hurting my feelings, because I don't want you to—"

"Addie!" Nick interrupted her with a shout. "Quit bossing me around!"

Addie clamped her mouth shut and Nick grinned. "There," he said. "Are you satisfied?"

He stood up to pedal into the wind, and they raced the rest of the way home.

* * *

"This could be a problem." Mr. McCormick studied the second clue and sighed. "Do you know how many bridges there are around here?" he asked his daughter.

"But it has to be a bridge near the Danners' property," Addie said. "It would be a bridge the brothers played at a lot. Like Nick and I play at the creek."

"The Little Vermilion River runs through all the property south of Danners'," Mr. McCormick told her. "Every time it crosses a road, there's a bridge. Are you going to search under all of them?"

"Which ones are closest to the Danners' house?"

Mr. McCormick pondered the question for a minute. "We really need to see a map of the area," he finally said. "The township has plats of all the land at the village hall. We could run in to Mt. Pilot and see if there's anyone in the office this afternoon."

Mrs. McCormick smiled fondly at her husband. "I think you're enjoying this scavenger hunt as much as the kids are."

Her husband grinned. "It is kind of fun. Besides, what better way is there to learn about the area where you live? Search for hidden treasure all over the county!"

Nick sniffed. "I wouldn't exactly call these things treasure," he said.

Mrs. McCormick frowned and took the small figure from Nick's hand. "This reminds me of something, but I can't remember what. I feel like I should know what it is. Oh, well. Maybe it will come to me. While you're in town, why don't you stop by the store and get something for dessert tonight?"

After promising to bring back rocky road ice cream, Mr. McCormick and the two children drove to the village hall in Mt. Pilot. There was no one in the office, but a village board member, Dan Lewis, was across the hall in the water department. He had a key to the main office and was more than happy to help them.

"Just where are you looking for these bridges?" he asked.

"Anywhere south of the old Danner home, the one that got blown away in the tornado," Mr. McCormick told him. "Ron Kleiss farms all that land. I'm not sure who owns it."

Mr. Lewis unlocked the main office and led them around a corner to a large table. He pulled an over-sized, leather-bound book from a shelf above the table and opened it to Section 30-H.

"I don't know who owns it either, but here's the property you're talking about," he said and pointed to a large map with sections marked off in squares and each square marked with a number. "This is where the homestead was." He pointed to a square in the northeast corner of the map. "Ron farms all this now," he made a sweeping gesture through six or seven of the sections, "and here's the Little Vermilion." His finger traced a long, dark line that squiggled through the bottom of the map.

"Where are the bridges?" Addie asked.

Mr. Lewis shook his head. "I guess they're not marked on this map," he said. "Maybe they're on the drainage map. That's in the conference room." He put the leather book back on the shelf, and they all left the office. He locked the door behind them.

"Why are you interested in these bridges?" he asked as they walked down the hall to the meeting room. Several people were on their way upstairs to the town's library.

"We found an old metal box that came from the Danner house when it was destroyed by the tornado," Addie began as he unlocked the door to the meeting room.

She went on to detail the rest of their story as they walked through a large, L-shaped room. Mr. Lewis led them around the L, to the far end of the room. Addie finished her story just as they stopped before a large wall map.

"Here's the Danner property," Mr. Lewis said. He pointed to an enlarged version of the section they'd just seen in the plat book. "And here's the Little Vermilion. This just might be the bridge where your next clue is hidden."

A soft sneeze, followed by a single thump, startled them all. Then there was a brief silence, followed by a series of thumps.

"Who's there?" Mr. Lewis called.

No one answered, but they could all hear the soft pad of footsteps in the main corridor.

Addie and Nick sped down the length of the room and around the corner. They ran out the door just in time to see a short, stocky girl with long blond hair disappear up the stairs to the library.

CHAPTER 5

The Girl with
the Long Blond Hair

Mr. Lewis and Mr. McCormick came around the corner of the meeting room just as Addie and Nick came back in. A table on the wall next to the door held several tall, spiral binders, and they had all fallen over. That was the *thump-thump-thump-thump* they had heard.

"Who was it?" Mr. Lewis asked the children.

"Just some girl," Nick answered.

Mr. Lewis stood the binders up and pushed the bookend back in place. "Everything seems to be in order," he said. "She probably just got curious when she saw the door open. No harm done."

He turned to Mr. McCormick. "Did that help, or would you like to look at the map again?"

Mr. McCormick shook his head. "No need. That helped a lot. Now we won't be driving all over the countryside looking under every bridge in the township. Thanks for your time."

Nick and Addie echoed their thanks. Mr. Lewis locked up the meeting room and returned to his business in the water department.

"Can we check out the bridge this afternoon, Dad?" They stepped outside into the warm spring air and waited on the corner as two vans and a truck turned the corner.

For some reason, Addie glanced up at the second-story windows of the village hall. "Nick, look!" she whispered. There was a girl staring at them out of the library window. She had long blond hair.

Nick recognized the hair too. He wagged his finger at her in a *shame on you!* manner and she disappeared.

Mr. McCormick hadn't noticed the girl. "Sure, I'll run you out there before we go home. But that's it for today. I've got work to do."

Addie hooked her arm through his and squeezed his hand. "Okay. Thanks."

The bridge they had seen on the map was almost a mile directly south of the Danner property. Mr. McCormick pulled the car off the road just north of the bridge, and they walked the rest of the way.

Addie and Nick hurried down the bank to the Little Vermilion. Addie slipped out of her sneakers, and Nick had his shoes off and was working on his socks when Mr. McCormick called to Addie.

"Got your flashlight, kiddo?"

Addie pulled the flashlight out of her back pocket. Nick grimaced.

"I left mine in the root cellar," he said.

"You can go back and get it later," Mr. McCormick told him. "Take a look at this," he said. "I'm afraid it's the end of your scavenger hunt, kids." He shone the light under the bridge, on something written in the concrete above their heads. Addie could see the numbers 8-8-80.

"What does that mean?" Nick asked.

"It's a date," Addie told him, her voice rough with disappointment. "The bridge was rebuilt in 1980."

Nick slapped his socks against his leg several times. "Oh, well," he finally said.

They peered inside the abutment anyway, but the concrete was smooth and there was no evidence of a "slot" anywhere. Addie slipped back into her sneakers. Nick flung his socks over his shoulder and carried his shoes back to the car.

No one spoke much on the way home. When Mr. McCormick stopped the car in their drive, he reached over to pat Addie's knee. "Sorry, kiddo," he said.

Addie gave him a small smile. "It's okay, Dad. I really appreciate you helping us as much as you did."

"Yeah," Nick echoed. "My dad thought we were all a little bonkers when I told him what we were doing." Nick's dad was nice, but he didn't have much of an imagination.

Addie's father laughed. "He's probably right. But that's okay. I've been called worse things than bonkers."

Mr. McCormick went inside, and Addie and Nick wandered into the backyard. Addie slipped into the tire swing that hung from the huge silver maple behind the house. Nick sat down on the edge of the sandbox and dug his bare toes into the warm sand.

"Well, that was the shortest adventure we've ever had," he said.

Addie swayed gently in the swing, spinning around at the same time. "Maybe that wasn't the right bridge."

"Give it up, Addie."

"Dad said there are lots of bridges in the township," she protested.

"Why would they hide something under a bridge miles away from their home?" Nick asked. "You were the one who said it had to be close to their property, and that bridge was the closest one."

Addie couldn't argue with that, so she swung harder, arching out over the sandbox. She came within inches of Nick's head, and he pushed the tire away. When it swung back, Nick grabbed it and tried to dump his friend on the ground. Addie put up a fight and finally broke free of his grip.

"So what are we going to do this afternoon?" she asked and swung back over the sandbox. "We can't even go to the creek."

Nick tried to ignore her, but when she gave him a gentle nudge with the toe of her shoe, he grabbed her foot and lifted it high above the ground. Addie slipped backwards through the tire and hung on to both sides, her bottom scraping the ground.

"I'm sorry, I'm sorry!" she laughed, and Nick let go of her foot. But she couldn't pull herself back up through the tire, so she finally wiggled out bottom first and landed in an ungraceful heap underneath the swing.

Nick held the tire while Addie sat up and brushed the dirt off both elbows. "Maybe we could find another creek to go swimming in," he grinned. "You're filthy!"

Addie stared at her friend and Nick frowned.

"What?" he asked. "Why do you always look at me like I've said something brilliant and I never know what it is?"

"'Another creek,'" she repeated. "It's not really another creek, it's the same drainage ditch, but it has to go through the Danners' property too."

"What are you talking about?"

"We play at the creek where it goes under the road near your house," Addie explained. "Maybe the Danner boys played at the creek where it goes under a road near *their* house."

"But there's no bridge there."

"It wouldn't have to be a real bridge," Addie said. "Just a 'span' where the ditch runs under a road."

Nick was still skeptical. "I think it's a wild goose chase," he said.

"Please, Nick," Addie said. "Let's go back to the place we found the truck. We'll follow the creek through the property Mr. Kleiss farms. If we don't find a bridge of some kind near the old homestead, I'll give up. Please?"

Nick began putting on his shoes and socks. "Nothing better to do," he said.

Addie ran to the kitchen door. "Mom, we're going riding," she yelled through the screen door.

"Be back in an hour," her mother answered.

The two children sped down the road. They left their bikes at the creek and walked the same path they'd walked the day before. They came to the truck quickly this time.

"Dad called Ron Kleiss last night," Addie said. "He's going to pull that truck out Monday or Tuesday. I'd like to watch."

"Me too," Nick agreed.

They walked steadily through the fields, keeping the creek to their right. The barn and the demolished shed on the Danner property came into view, a quarter mile to the east. They kept walking and were soon south of the old homestead.

"How much farther, Addie?" Nick wanted to know.

"I don't know," Addie said. She glanced at her watch. They'd been walking about fifteen minutes. They could walk for fifteen more minutes before they had to turn around to make it home in their allotted hour.

"Look!" Nick pointed to a wide grassy strip that ran through the middle of the field. It crossed the drainage ditch about an eighth of a mile ahead.

Addie and Nick began to run. They slid down the embankment to the creek when they got to the grass road. Where the creek ran under the road was a very old wooden plank bridge.

Addie was ecstatic. "See what I meant?" she said to Nick. "This isn't a real road. The farmer uses it to get his equipment in and out of fields. Back when the Danners farmed, they probably used horses. That's why the clue said 'a span where horses trot.'"

Nick had his shoes and socks off once more, and he plunged into the icy cold water. Addie was right behind him. They splashed through the water to the bridge. It was even colder in the shade under the bridge.

The wooden structure beneath the road was sturdy but weather-beaten. The heavy beams provided any number of spots to stash a package, but Nick was discouraged.

"Addie, anything hidden here fifty years ago was bound to be blown away or washed out by now."

Addie shook her head. "No. The clue said 'careful searching will find the slot.' A slot is an opening to something, like a mail slot. They hid the package inside of something, somewhere."

"There aren't any slots down here," Nick muttered.

"You give up too quick. The clue said 'careful *searching*.' You haven't done any searching."

Nick splashed a handful of water up Addie's back and she shivered.

"Cut it out, Nick, that's cold. Help me look," she commanded. She heard the demanding tone of her own voice and gave her friend a quick grin. "Please help me look," she amended.

"Well, since you said please," Nick murmured. He crossed to the other side of the bridge and began running his hands up and down the heavy wooden beams. "So I'm looking for some kind of hole, huh?"

Addie was too busy examining her side of the bridge to answer. They searched in silence for several minutes. Nick was about to give up when Addie gave an excited shout.

"Here's . . . something," she said, reaching over her head. "There's a hole of some kind. You can hardly see the opening because it's so dark under here. Wait a minute. I can get my hand in . . . oh, yuk!" She squealed in dismay and pulled her hand out in a hurry. It was covered with cobwebs.

"Yuk, yuk, yuk," she cried and danced around in the water, trying to get the sticky threads off her fingers. "I hate spiders!"

Nick chortled at her discomfort. "What a wimp," he grinned. He found the hole and stuck his hand inside. "This only goes back about six inches . . . wait." He frowned. "The hole goes down, not back," he said.

He struggled for several moments to get his wrist and arm into the opening. He swallowed hard and gave a little shudder. "This is pretty gross," he admitted.

Then he shouted, "I found something!" He had his arm in the hole almost to his elbow, and he strained to get it in just a little bit farther. "I can't quite reach it. There! I've got it."

He bit his lip in concentration as he slowly pulled his arm back out. Addie held her breath until he pulled his find through the slot with his thumb and forefinger.

It was another oilskin package. "Yes!" Addie shouted.

Nick gave her the bag and stooped quickly to rinse off his arm and hand. "Yuk, yuk, yuk!" he said in a high, whiny voice, imitating Addie.

She ignored him and splashed over to the bank. She laid their prize in the grass and wiped her feet off before stepping back into her sneakers.

Addie waited for Nick to get his shoes back on, then they both ran up the embankment and took off through the field. They didn't even attempt to open the bag this time.

Addie slowed to a quick walk when they came in sight of the barn and shed. "Look, Nick. Someone's on the Danner property."

A dark red van sat in the drive near the old barn, and three people were walking in the yard.

Nick shrugged. "So what? Probably just curious trespassers like us. Come on, let's hurry."

He began to run again, and Addie took off after him. They got back to the road where they'd left their bikes and pulled them out of the weeds.

"My house or Miss T.'s?" Addie asked, trying to be diplomatic.

Nick grinned. "You're sure being polite," he said.

Addie frowned. "It's not going to last if you make fun of me. We're going to my house." Nick just laughed and followed her as she sped off down the road.

They'd almost reached Addie's house when a dark red van approached the two children from behind. It picked up speed, pulled into the left lane, and passed them. Addie and Nick caught just a glimpse of a young girl with long blond hair staring at them out the back window.

CHAPTER 6

Surprise!

"That's weird," Nick said. "Do you think she was following us?" He dropped his bike in Addie's yard and walked back to the road. He watched the van until it disappeared from view.

"Of course not," Addie said slowly, although the thought had occurred to her as well. It puzzled her, but only for a moment. She was too eager to open the package. She ran in the back door, and Nick followed her.

"Mom! Dad!" Addie bellowed. Her mother peered around the doorway of the living room, her finger to her lips. She was on the phone, listening to someone, a very pained expression on her face.

Addie began rummaging through the cabinet drawers, looking for a pair of scissors. She kept one ear tuned to the phone conversation.

"Yes, I understand," Mrs. McCormick said. "No, I'm sorry, I don't agree. . . . Yes, it is just my opinion, but I *am* entitled to one." She said this rather sharply, and Addie and Nick exchanged knowing glances.

"Mrs. Kreiling," Nick whispered loudly. Addie nodded.

Mrs. Kreiling was a woman from their church who had her own opinion about everything and everybody. If you didn't agree with her, you soon found out how wrong you were. She made sure to tell you.

Addie found the scissors just as Mr. McCormick walked into the kitchen. "What's up, kiddo?" His eyes widened in surprise when he saw the package on the table, and he began to laugh. "I don't believe this," he said with a chuckle. "Where did you find this one?"

Nick told Mr. McCormick of Addie's hunch about the creek while Addie struggled to cut open the tough material with dull scissors.

"Here, honey," Mr. McCormick said. "Those scissors need sharpening." He took the bag from his daughter and opened another drawer. He pulled out a utility knife and clicked the blade into place.

Meanwhile, Mrs. McCormick hung up the phone in the next room. She appeared in the kitchen, her eyes snapping. "That woman is—" she began.

"A child of God and your sister in Christ," Mr. McCormick finished for her with a grin.

His wife took a deep breath and closed her eyes. "A child of God and my sister in Christ," she repeated through clenched teeth.

"You might not agree with her, but you can meet her halfway," Mr. McCormick continued.

"I might not agree with her, but I can meet her halfway," Mrs. McCormick said. She sighed and opened her eyes. "You just keep telling me that, honey."

She smiled brightly at Addie. "What have we got here?" she asked. "I thought your father said the bridge was gone."

"Wrong bridge," Addie told her and explained her hunch about the creek once more. "And there it was, inside this slot, just like the clue said," she finished.

She glanced at Nick to see if he was going to tease her about the spider webs again, but Nick was busy. Mr. McCormick had placed a wooden cutting board on top of the cabinet. He was showing Nick how to use the knife, and Nick was trying not to cut his fingers off.

With Mr. McCormick's help, the young boy cut open the bag. Inside, as they suspected, was another wooden figure. It was similar to the first, with square shoulders, no arms, and a round wooden head with a stub protruding from the top. But this one was decorated, and the effect was comical.

Brown hair had been painted around the stub and down the sides of his head. He had rock eyes, although one rock was missing, and his smile had been whittled in, complete with two front teeth. Blue overalls were painted on the chest and legs, with two bare feet painted in at the bottom. Much of the color around the bottom had worn or chipped off.

"Tom Sawyer," Addie said immediately and Nick nodded.

"Or some other country bumpkin," he said. He hesitated for a moment, then asked, "Can I take him home and show my folks?"

"No." Addie spoke before she thought.

"Why not?" Nick protested. "It's not like you own him. I just want to show my mom and dad what we've found."

Addie had no good reason to keep from sharing their find with Nick's parents, and she knew her parents were staring at her.

"I just think we should keep everything together in the metal box," she mumbled.

"*I* found the metal box," Nick reminded her. "And I'm the one who pulled this guy out of the spider webs," he added under his breath.

Addie's father was watching her, a slight frown on his face. "It's only fair to let Nick's family share in the fun," he said. "Let's pack everything up in the metal box, and I'll drive it over to the Bradys when Nick's ready to go home."

Addie bit her lip to keep from protesting and she nodded. "All right," she said quietly.

Her father reached over and kissed the top of her head softly. "You can't always be in control, kiddo," he said softly.

Addie jerked back in surprise and stared at her father. She glanced at Nick, but he was staring at the floor. Tears burned her eyes and she swallowed hard. Did her own father think she was bossy too?

"Besides," Mr. McCormick said cheerfully, "aren't you both forgetting something?"

Addie couldn't answer. Nick looked up from the floor and shrugged. "What?"

Mr. McCormick picked up the bag and reached inside. He drew out a familiar-looking yellowed slip of paper and grinned. "The next clue."

"Oh, yeah," Nick said and even Addie perked up. Her father read the words out loud.

> We raise our voice in celebration,
> In a style so free and grand,
> When we celebrate our nation,
> Even Nellie takes a stand.

When he finished, the kitchen was completely silent. Addie took the piece of paper and read the words to herself, with Nick looking over her shoulder. She read the verse several times. This one made no sense at all.

"It must have something to do with the Fourth of July," Nick offered.

Addie nodded. "But it doesn't make any mention of a location. And who's Nellie?"

Mr. McCormick grinned. "It looks like this one's going to take a little bit more thinking, Sherlock."

He brought the metal box and its contents to the kitchen and set it on the table. They packed the two wooden figures and the clues inside with the rest of the toys and the scarlet box and closed the lid.

"Do you want to ride with me to the Bradys?" Addie's father asked her, but she shook her head.

Nick paused on his way out the kitchen door. "Thanks, Addie," he said.

Addie just shrugged and nodded. Why was he thanking her? It wasn't her choice. "Don't let Jesse Kate get hold of them," she said briefly, referring to Nick's little sister.

Nick grinned. "Give me credit for some brains," he joked, and Addie finally smiled. "I'll give them back to you at church tomorrow," he said.

"Okay," Addie replied.

She watched Mr. McCormick drive away. Nick followed on his bike, and she watched until he disappeared in the late afternoon sun. She walked slowly up to her room and flopped down on the bed.

You can't always be in control, kiddo. Her father's words echoed Nick's feelings and fresh tears sprang to Addie's eyes. She knew they were both right.

I'm sorry, Lord, she prayed. *I know it's selfish to expect my friends to do everything my way all the time. But—* She stopped herself, not wanting to make excuses to the Lord. *Please teach me how to . . . ,* Addie struggled for the right word, *. . . compromise. In Jesus' name, Amen.*

Addie sighed deeply. Usually she looked forward to seeing God answer prayer. She had a feeling this answer wasn't going to come easy.

* * *

Addie had her first opportunity to learn the art of compromise the next morning after church. She and her parents went to brunch with Nick and his family. Waiting for their meal in the pancake house, the conversation naturally turned to the children's latest adventure. Mr. Brady was not particularly impressed with their box of toys, but Mrs. Brady was delighted with it all.

"Addie, I'd love to use the toys in a painting," she said. She had been an art major in college. "I'd use my grandmother's quilt—it's over a hundred years old—as a backdrop. I'll sit Jesse Kate in the middle, with the toys spread around her."

At the mention of Jesse Kate, Addie's eyes grew wide and Mrs. Brady laughed. "Oh, I never use her as a live model. She can't hold still that long. So I take a picture of her and paint from the picture. I'll put her in first and paint the toys in later."

Addie breathed a sigh of relief. Then she nodded. "I think that would be pretty," she agreed.

"Great!" Mrs. Brady beamed. "I'm going to start painting this afternoon. If you find any more of those figures, I'll add them later."

"You won't find anymore," Mr. Brady said in a matter-of-fact tone. "You're bound to run out of luck sooner or later. There's no way all of those packages survived after fifty years."

Nick frowned at his father, and Mrs. Brady poked her husband. "Don't be such a spoilsport," she chided him. "They've done great so far. Be a little more supportive."

Mr. Brady only shrugged and changed the subject to something more interesting—the Dow Jones average. While their parents discussed stocks and bonds and futures and commodities, Addie and Nick kept Jesse Kate entertained.

"Thanks, Addie," Nick said. "I promise I'll keep an eye on everything. Mom said she's going to set the painting up in her studio." The Bradys' laundry room doubled as Mrs. Brady's studio, and Jesse was never allowed in there.

"It's okay," Addie assured him. "You have as much right to keep the toys as I do."

Nick gave his friend a surprised look but said nothing.

Addie decided to be honest. "Okay, I'd rather keep them at my house. But I prayed last night and asked the Lord to teach me how to compromise. I know I can't always have my own way. So maybe this is His first test. Maybe He wants to see if I really meant what I said."

Nick grinned and looked heavenward. "Let me know if You need any help, Lord," he said.

After a huge meal of pancakes, eggs, bacon, sausage, toast, and juice, the adults settled back for a final cup of coffee. Mrs. Brady dug through her purse for several broken crayons, and Jesse Kate scribbled on the back of her placemat while Addie and Nick played hangman on theirs. Addie won the first round when Nick couldn't guess the word *calculator*.

Then it was Nick's turn. Spelling was his least favorite subject, so he always chose fairly simple words that Addie usually guessed after three or four letters. Today she had the letters s__p_ise and was ready to guess the word when she looked up and saw several people approaching their table.

A small, thin woman with soft gray hair and round glasses stopped at Mr. McCormick's chair. Behind her was a young boy, about Addie and Nick's age. He was as tall as the woman, with serious blue eyes and a blond crewcut. Behind him stood a young girl. She had long blond hair and she stared at Addie and Nick. They stared back.

The woman held out her hand to Mr. McCormick. He rose to his feet and shook it. "Please sit down," she said in a nervous voice and glanced at the children behind her.

"I'm very sorry to disturb you, but you see, my granddaughter Emily said, you see, that you were interested in, I mean—" She stopped and took a deep breath.

"Let me start over. My name is Sarah Tyler. You don't know me, but my parents were Stella and Sidney Danner. Have you ever heard of them?"

CHAPTER 7

Chadwick and Emily

Mr. McCormick stared at the tiny woman. Mrs. McCormick nearly choked on a swallow of coffee. Sarah Tyler smiled nervously.

"I'm sorry," Mr. McCormick said. "This is quite a surprise. Yes, we've definitely heard of the Danner family. I don't think we've talked about much else for the last two days." He smiled and glanced at Addie and Nick, but they weren't smiling. They were staring at Emily.

"Won't you have a seat?" he asked and then checked himself. There were no seats to be had, and the restaurant was getting more and more crowded, with several families sitting in the waiting area.

Emily pulled on her grandmother's arm and whispered something in her ear. Mrs. Tyler nodded.

"We've finished eating and it looks like you're done as well. Would you like to go across the street to the park? Maybe we could talk there," she suggested.

"That's a great idea," Mr. McCormick agreed. He and Nick's father split the bill, and Mr. Brady paid at the cash register.

"We need to get Jesse home for her nap," Mrs. Brady said with an apologetic smile. "We're not really the ones you need to talk to, anyway," she told Mrs. Tyler. "Gwen and John have been helping the kids with . . . well, they'll explain all that to you," she said.

Addie's folks agreed to drop Nick off at home after their conversation with Sarah Tyler, and the Bradys left, with Jesse Kate wailing at the top of her lungs. She'd gotten very attached to Nick in the last few months, an honor he didn't especially appreciate.

The children walked out of the restaurant ahead of the adults. Emily and her brother walked side by side a few steps ahead of Nick and Addie. Once in the park, the boy seemed to debate between two picnic tables and finally chose the one nearest the grandstand in the center of the park.

Emily sat on one side and her brother slid in next to her, but he didn't sit down. He waited for Nick and Addie to join them, then he extended his hand to Nick.

"My name is Chadwick," he said solemnly and shook Nick's hand.

Nick glanced at Addie out of the corner of his eye. "My name is Nicholas," Nick said in an equally somber tone, and Addie almost laughed.

Emily sniffed. "Nobody calls you Chadwick," she said to her brother. "Just Chad," she told Nick and Addie. "And I'm Emily."

"Just Nick," Nick said with a grin.

"I'm Addie."

The four children stared at one another, then Chad spoke again.

"My full name is Chadwick Sebastian Tyler, the third," he said without cracking a smile. "If I expect to be addressed as such when I'm practicing law, I need to establish a precedent for said use early in my career."

Nick cocked one eyebrow and fixed the other boy with a disbelieving stare. "What?"

Emily just groaned and pulled her brother down next to her on the bench. "Don't pay any attention to him," she told Nick and Addie. "Our father's a lawyer and Chad tries to talk like him," she said.

"I'll be studying pre-law in college," Chad told them.

"If you make it through junior high math," Emily said. "And that's a big if," she told Nick and Addie. "Dad did most of his homework this year."

Chad blushed and glared at his younger sister, but she ignored him. Addie's parents and Mrs. Tyler joined the children at the picnic table, and Emily scooted over to make room for her grandmother.

When the adults were seated, Mr. McCormick spoke first.

"Over the past two days, Addie and Nick have found several items we think came from the Danner homestead, or belonged to the Danner brothers," he said. "Before we examined these items, we found out a little bit about your family history. We knew Stella and Sidney Danner died in the early forties. And your uncle was declared missing in action in World War II."

"We also knew Stella died from complications after childbirth," Mrs. McCormick continued. "But it never occurred to us to look for her child." She paused. "That's you," she said to Mrs. Tyler, and the older woman nodded.

"We're very sorry," Mr. McCormick said. "It was careless of us to assume there were no heirs. These items are really very unique family heirlooms. We can get them this afternoon and bring them to you if you'll just give us your address."

Addie sucked in her breath sharply and stared at her father, but he appeared not to notice.

Mrs. Tyler was shaking her head and smiling. "Please don't feel bad. I was ecstatic when Emily told me she'd ... oh, wait. I'm getting ahead of myself. Let me give you a little of my background.

"You know my father died before I was born, and my mother shortly after. My mother's sister raised me, so I grew up Sarah Morgan, not Sarah Danner. I doubt if there are many people left who remember my biological parents. It would have been difficult to find me, even if you'd tried."

"How did you find us?" Mrs. McCormick asked.

Mrs. Tyler smiled wryly and slipped an arm around the young girl next to her. "Emily is my sweetest granddaughter—"

"She's your only granddaughter," Chad interrupted under his breath.

"—but she has a tendency to be a little nosy," Mrs. Tyler explained. "She saw you in the library yesterday and heard you talking with another man about the Danner property."

Emily spoke up in her own defense. "After the tornado took the old house, Granny was upset. When I heard you talking about something you found on the Danner property, I felt like Granny should know about it, so I followed you into that big room and . . . listened."

"Eavesdropped," Chad interrupted again.

"Well, I'm glad you did." Mr. McCormick smiled at Emily. "And *you'll* be glad you did when you see what Addie and Nick have found."

Addie felt a sinking feeling in the pit of her stomach, but she tried to dismiss it. Mrs. Tyler smiled at her in eager anticipation.

"Please tell me," the older woman said. "Just what have you found?"

"We found a big metal box submerged in the creek by my house." Nick jumped into the conversation without hesitation. "It had several handmade toys in it and—"

"But what about the clues?" Emily interrupted.

Addie stared at her in surprise.

"You were telling that guy at the village hall about a clue under a bridge somewhere," Emily persisted and Addie nodded.

"There was a letter," she said slowly. "A letter to Frank."

"Frank is my father's younger brother," Mrs. Tyler said.

"The letter said . . ." Addie paused and thought hard. " 'I'm sorry I can't be there to go on the scavenger hunt with you this time,' " she repeated from memory.

"The first clue to the scavenger hunt was with the letter," Nick said. "So we figured it out and found this little wooden guy in the root cellar on the Danner property."

"There was a second clue in the root cellar," Addie continued. "That clue led to the bridge. We found another wooden man under the bridge, and another clue."

Emily and Chad were both wide-eyed and staring at Nick and Addie. "So where did the third clue lead?" Emily prodded.

Nick frowned. "We haven't been able to figure this one out. It doesn't make any sense at all."

Addie looked thoughtfully at Mrs. Tyler. "You might understand it, though," she said. "It seems to be about some event that Frank and Sidney would both remember."

Mrs. Tyler shook her head. "I'd like to think I could help, but I never knew my father." Then she snapped her fingers. "But I do have one of his journals! It never meant much to me because I didn't know the people or places or events he wrote about. I'll read through it again."

"Is that all you have left of your parents?" Addie asked.

Mrs. Tyler nodded. "There were other things—lots of them. Books, furniture, clothes, dishes. But when the tornado took the house, everything was ruined."

Addie was puzzled. "That house has been abandoned for years," she said.

"Oh, I know," said Mrs. Tyler.

"Why did you leave things that were important to you in an abandoned house?" Nick asked bluntly.

"Because it was locked up tighter than a drum after the end of World War II."

Nick was confused. "Don't you have a key?" he said.

Emily giggled and Nick looked insulted. "It's not Granny's house," she said.

"Then whose is it?" Nick wanted to know.

"When my father and mother both died, ownership of the house and farm passed to my Uncle Frank," Mrs. Tyler said.

"But he's dead," Addie protested.

Mrs. Tyler looked with surprise at the young girl and shook her head. "Oh, no. Whatever gave you that idea? Uncle Frank is very much alive. He lives just north of here."

Mr. McCormick shook his head. "Another careless assumption on our part," he said to his wife and the two children. "Not all soldiers missing in action were dead. Many of them came home, like Frank Danner."

"Then, technically," Addie said slowly, "the box and all its contents belong to Frank."

Mrs. Tyler nodded. "And I'd love to give them to him. But Uncle Frank has only spoken to me twice in my entire life. And he told me, in no uncertain terms, that the second time would be the last."

"But you're his niece," Nick protested.

"I'm also a reminder of a very unhappy part of his past. When he came back from the war, Stella and Sidney had both died. So he boarded up the house and moved north. As far as I know, he's never been back. He just rents the land to another farmer," Mrs. Tyler said. "I don't think he'd be pleased if he knew you'd found those toys."

"So we won't tell him," Emily said promptly.

"We should be prepared for possible legal repercussions," Chad murmured.

Mr. and Mrs. McCormick glanced at the serious young boy, and Mrs. Tyler patted his hand. "Why don't you worry about that for us, dear," she said lightly.

"I can't wait to see the third clue," Emily exclaimed.

Nick and Addie exchanged an uneasy glance, and the sinking feeling in the pit of Addie's stomach returned.

"I'll read the journal tonight, and Chad and I can start searching first thing tomorrow morning," she said happily.

CHAPTER 8

Who's Really
in Charge?

"Emily," Mrs. Tyler said gently, "aren't you forgetting something?"

Emily thought for a moment, then shook her head. "What?"

"Addie and Nick have done all the work up to this point. I think you should ask them if you may join in their search."

Addie let out the breath she'd been holding, and she felt Nick relax beside her.

Chad was not pleased. "As the great-grandchildren of Sidney and Stella Danner," he began, "Emily and I have the option of—"

"Oh, shut up, Chad," Emily said rudely. "It's not like anybody's going to sue anybody. We're only kids. But they were our relatives, and it's our box and our scavenger hunt."

She folded her arms across her chest and glared across the table at Addie and Nick.

Addie felt a bubble of anger rise up in her throat, but before she could say anything, her father put a restraining hand on her arm.

"We're certainly not going to insist that Addie and Nick continue on this hunt," he said mildly. "If we can't work something out, we'll return the box to you with our best wishes."

Addie wanted to shake off her father's arm and shout, *Over my dead body!* in Emily's face. But she knew that would end any hopes they had of continuing in the scavenger hunt. So she pressed her lips together and stared at the graffiti scratched on the picnic table.

"Emily Tyler," her grandmother said firmly, "I want you to apologize to Addie and Nick right now."

Emily stared defiantly at her grandmother for several seconds, then lowered her eyes. "I'm sorry," she said.

Mrs. Tyler's expression softened. "I can't insist the four of you work together on this scavenger hunt. Emily and Chad are only visiting for two weeks, and I want our time together to be enjoyable," she told Mr. and Mrs. McCormick.

Emily threw a triumphant glance at Addie and Nick. Her grandmother saw it and frowned. "However, if you *can't* agree on how to proceed, we'll pick up the box and its contents, and I'll donate everything in it to the Historical Society."

All four children turned to stare at Mrs. Tyler.

"You mean, no one gets to search for the next clue?" Emily asked.

"That's right."

Emily swallowed hard and clamped her mouth shut.

"You can't always have your own way, honey," her grandmother said gently. "You have to learn to compromise."

Addie felt a smile tugging at the corners of her mouth, but she knew Emily might see her and misunderstand, so she smothered it quickly.

She decided to make the first show of compromise. "Nick and I don't think of this as our search, anyway," she said. "We'd be glad to have help on the next clue. It's a tough one."

Nick was staring at her in surprise, but she ignored him and went on. "The first two wooden figures were hidden on the Danner property. I don't think the third one is. This clue talks about celebrating our nation. We think it might have something to do with the Fourth of July. A celebration like that would have been here in town."

Despite their annoyance, Emily and Chad were listening with growing interest. Addie went on.

"If you look through your great-grandfather's journal tonight, maybe you'll find some reference to a celebration. We could go from there."

Chad was nodding. "I think this can be worked out in the best interests of everyone concerned," he said.

Emily was still frowning and tracing the words KAREN LOVES JIM carved in the cross grain of the picnic table.

"What do you say, Emily?" Nick asked casually.

Emily looked up and gave Nick and Addie a rueful smile. "That sounds okay to me. I . . . I guess I didn't really think about how you would feel," she admitted. "I wouldn't like it if someone else barged in on my scavenger hunt either."

"That's my girl!" her grandmother exclaimed, and she gave her granddaughter a big hug. "I think you'll all have a lot of fun."

"Can we get the box and the clues tonight?" Emily asked hopefully.

"Of course," Mr. McCormick said. "Right now, everything is at Nick's house. Nick's mother is an artist and she wanted to do a painting of the toys," he explained.

Mrs. Tyler gasped in delight. "What a wonderful idea! Do you think I could persuade her to sell it when she's finished?"

"Not unless you really like my baby sister," Nick joked. "She's going to be smack dab in the middle of it."

"Donna's an excellent artist," Mrs. McCormick said. "I'm sure you could commission her to do a second painting."

Emily sighed. "I was hoping we could take the toys home today."

Her grandmother gave her a warning smile. "Now, dear, you don't really need those toys. If Nick's mother has started her painting, we're not going to disturb them."

Addie spoke up. "You can take the clues," she said. "I'll make a copy of the last one before you take it. That way all of us can study it tonight."

"Why don't we follow you to Nick's?" Mrs. Tyler suggested. "I'd like to take another look at the Danner homestead while we're in that area."

They left the park and walked back across the street to the parking lot of the pancake house. Nick and Addie climbed in the backseat of the station wagon, and Mr. McCormick led the way out of town.

Once Mr. McCormick turned the radio on, Addie and Nick discussed the new turn of events in low voices.

"How do you think this is going to work?" Nick asked Addie glumly.

She shrugged. "We'll see," she said.

"You don't think it's going to work any better than I do," Nick stated.

Addie didn't deny it. All she said was, "We've got to try, Nick. What other choice do we have?"

"You're right," he agreed. "But I don't have to like it, do I?"

When they got to the Bradys', Donna was in her "studio" mixing colors. She was delighted to talk with Mrs. Tyler about doing a painting for the older woman and refused to take any money for it.

"I can't promise how soon I'll get it done," she laughed. "Besides, if I can use the toys in a painting with Jesse, that's payment enough."

While the women talked at length about design and color, the men retired to the den to watch the

Windy City Classic between the White Sox and the Cubs.

Nick carried the metal box into the kitchen and got a notebook and pencil from the cabinet. He gave the clues to Emily and Chad and the notebook to Addie. She copied the third clue on paper, mostly from memory.

While she was writing, Emily and Chad studied the first two clues. Nick explained in detail how they had found the wooden men behind the bricks in the root cellar and in the slot under the bridge. When he finished, Chad and Emily were properly impressed.

"That's excellent deductive reasoning," Chad said.

Addie tried not to smile, but Emily saw her reaction and kicked Chad's shoe. "Would you stop it?" she demanded.

"Stop what?" Chad asked innocently.

"He's going to drive you nuts," she told Nick and Addie. "Dad showed him one of his notebooks from the first pre-law course he took in college, and Chad's been talking like a textbook ever since."

Chad was unperturbed. "I'm simply trying to improve my vocabulary and develop my thinking skills," he said.

"Why don't you try working on your social skills?" Emily muttered, and Nick began to laugh.

Addie kicked *his* shoe and changed the subject. "Do you have any ideas about what the last clue means?" she asked the brother and sister.

Emily read the verse out loud. "'We raise our voice in celebration, in a style so free and grand, when we celebrate our nation, even Nellie takes a stand.'"

"It's clear Nellie is an important operative in this equation," Chad said.

"English, please," Nick snapped.

"We gotta find out who Nellie is," Emily translated. "And why is she taking a stand?"

"To take a stand means to let people know what you believe," Addie said. "Even Nellie 'takes a stand' when they 'celebrate the nation.'" She sighed. "I sure hope there's something in that journal that will shed some light on this one."

"Maybe you can bring the journal with you when we . . . when we . . ." Nick stopped.

"When we what?" Emily asked.

"I don't know," Nick said. "How are we going to work together on this? Are you going to come out to Addie's or are we going to come to your place?"

Chad answered. "I believe the burden falls on you to come to our—"

Nick couldn't take it any longer. "Would you talk like a normal kid?" he demanded. "How old are you, anyway?"

Chad was shocked into silence but only for a second. "I'm . . . twelve in four months."

"Which means you're eleven," Nick said. "Same as us. So act like it, okay?"

"Nick, quiet down." Addie shushed him with an anxious glance toward the studio.

"I want this arrangement to work as much as anybody else," he said, "but if I have to listen to Perry Mason all day I'll go berserk."

Chad regarded Nick with contempt. "If you want to be a part of this scavenger hunt, you don't have much choice."

"The hunt's off if we don't work together," Nick reminded him.

"Not for us it isn't," Chad said.

"Your grandmother won't let you—"

"She won't know," Chad interrupted. "Granny lets Emmie and me do pretty much what we want during the day. As long as we check in every hour or so, she never asks questions."

Addie and Nick were staring at Chad in disbelief.

"We already have the next clue," he continued. "We've got everything we need. We *don't* need you."

"We've got the clue too," Nick stammered.

"But what does it mean?" Chad asked him. "You don't have any idea."

"Neither do you!" Addie protested, her voice rising in anger.

"We've got the journal."

Addie choked back her frustration, and Nick stared at Chad with such fury in his eyes the other boy took a step backwards. Then he turned to leave the room.

"If you want to stay in this," Chad said over his shoulder, "you'd better remember who's really in charge."

CHAPTER 9

Will It Work?

Emily watched her older brother leave the room. She turned back to Nick and Addie. Her face was pink, and it was difficult for her to look them in the eye.

"I'm sorry," she said. "Chad can be a—" Emily paused.

Addie filled in the sentence in her mind. *A brat.*

"—a brat sometimes," Emily finished. "He's always been real smart, just never very friendly. Kids tease him all the time at school. Mom says he hides behind big words so he won't have to talk to anyone."

"It works great," Nick said. "I sure don't want to talk to him."

Emily looked dismayed. "Chad will cool down by tomorrow," she said. "Please don't tell Granny you had a fight."

"We won't," Addie assured her. "Nick and Chad can work this out after they've *both* cooled down."

Nick frowned at Addie, and she frowned right back.

"Let's ask my mom if she can bring Nick and me in town tomorrow," Addie continued, motioning to the younger girl.

They left the kitchen, and Nick trailed after them. The three women were still in the studio, arranging and rearranging the toys on the quilt. Mrs. Brady was very particular about her paintings. She was always talking about "composition" and "flow."

Addie waited for a break in their conversation. There was none. "Mom," she finally interrupted in a soft voice, and her mother looked up.

"Ready to go?" she asked.

"Almost," Addie said. "If it's all right with Mrs. Tyler, can Nick and I go in town tomorrow to look for the next clue with Emily and Chad?"

Mrs. Tyler heard the question and smiled. "It's just fine with me," she said. "Having friends to play with will certainly make these two weeks fun for Chad and Emmie," she beamed.

Mr. McCormick joined them in the doorway of the laundry room. He heard the exchange and told his wife, "I've got an appointment at the accountant's at nine tomorrow morning. I could put their bikes in the back of the station wagon and drive them in."

"I'm taking Jesse to the doctor in the afternoon," Mrs. Brady said. "If you pack a lunch and eat in town, I can pick you up in the van after two."

"That sounds great," Mrs. Tyler said. "I live at 1484 Long Pond Road." She glanced at her watch. "Well, we have to leave. I want to drive by the old place before we go back to town, so we'd better get going."

She thanked Mrs. Brady once more, and everyone walked the older woman and her granddaughter outside to their van. Chad was waiting for them there, leaning against the side door and kicking up gravel.

"See you tomorrow, Emily," Addie said brightly, and the other girl waved.

Chad crawled into the van without a word, and Nick went back inside. If the adults noticed, they said nothing.

After the Tylers were gone, Mr. Brady joined them outside, and the adults stood around and talked some more. Addie went searching for Nick. He was in the den, listening to Harry Carey sing "Take Me Out to the Ballgame."

"Hey, Nick," Addie said, "we'll pick you up about 8:30 tomorrow morning, okay?"

"Yeah, sure."

Addie turned to leave, but Nick stopped her.

"I can't believe you're going along with that jerk," he said.

When Addie didn't answer, Nick persisted. "Do you *really* want to spend the first day of summer vacation taking orders from that little dictator?"

"No," Addie said sharply, "but I really want to keep looking for these clues. It's important to me. Besides," she went on, "maybe God's trying to teach me how to compromise—with Chad."

"Chad might have a big vocabulary," Nick told her, "but he doesn't know the meaning of the word *compromise*. He'll walk all over you."

Nick's words bothered Addie, because she was afraid they were true. But all she said was, "We'll see."

* * *

When the McCormicks arrived home, Addie ran upstairs to change her clothes. She had just slipped into her favorite pair of jeans and a sweatshirt when there was a knock at her door.

"Come on in," she called, and her father poked his head into the room.

"Hi, kiddo. Can I talk to you for a minute?"

"Sure, Dad," she said.

Mr. McCormick pulled out the chair at Addie's desk and nodded toward the bed. "You'd better hang that dress up."

Addie made a face but did as she was told. Usually it was her mom who hassled her about hanging up clothes. She got a hanger from the closet and forced it down the neck of the dress, then shoved the dress in the closet between some pants and blouses.

When she was finished, Mr. McCormick nodded toward the bed again. Addie sat down.

Mr. McCormick got right to the point. "Is this going to work?"

Addie avoided his eyes. "Sure it is."

"Addie . . ."

The young girl sighed. "Chad thinks he's in charge. Nick's not too happy about it."

Her father nodded. "I thought there was some tension between those two when we left. So Nick's not happy about it. What about you?"

Addie studied a loose thread in the comforter on her bed. "I think it will be okay," she said.

She could feel her father's eyes on her, and she looked at the thread a little closer. It really needed to be cut with the scissors.

"Addie . . ." Her father reached out and poked her leg with the toe of his shoe. "Maybe you think you can fool me. But can you talk yourself into believing that? Because if you can't, there's going to be problems."

Addie thought about her father's words for a few seconds. Then she looked him in the eye. "I'm not too happy about it either," she admitted.

Mr. McCormick nodded. "I thought not. I know how important it is to you to keep going on this scavenger hunt, hon. Even I'd be disappointed if you had to quit now," he said with a smile. "But you'd better think about it. Is it worth it? I don't like to make snap judgments about people, but Chad and Emily both seem to be pretty strong-willed kids."

"So am I," Addie said. "So is Nick."

Mr. McCormick laughed. "That's exactly my point," he told her. "Four kids who all want to do things their own way aren't going to be much fun for one another."

Addie decided to tell her father about her prayer. "Do you remember what you told me yesterday afternoon? You said I can't always be in control."

Mr. McCormick nodded.

"Nick told me the same thing yesterday morning. I decided the Lord must be trying to tell me something if both of you think I'm too bossy."

Mr. McCormick crossed over to the bed and sat down next to his daughter. "I don't think bossy is quite the right word, kiddo," he said as he put an arm around Addie's shoulders. "I do think you need to learn how to compromise a little bit more."

"Exactly," Addie said with some excitement. "That's what I prayed! I asked God to teach me how to compromise. Maybe working with Chad and Emily will be my first lesson."

Mr. McCormick took a deep breath and studied his serious young daughter. He smiled tenderly. "Maybe it will be, sweetheart." He hesitated.

Addie grinned. "You always told me to be careful what I pray. I just might get what I asked for."

He laughed. "I think you have. More than you realize." Then he became serious. "Do you know what compromise means, Addie?"

Addie looked surprised. "I think so. You let other people have their way sometimes."

Mr. McCormick shook his head. "Not exactly. It means you listen to the other person's point of view.

If his opinion is just as reasonable as yours, and he's not asking you to do something you know is wrong, then you can compromise. You give up a little bit of what you want so that the other person can have a little bit of what they want "

Addie thought carefully. "In other words, don't let someone talk you into doing something wrong and call it compromise."

Her father nodded. "And there's one more thing," he said. "Compromise works both ways. It takes two people to compromise. If you're the only one willing to give up some of what you want, you're not compromising. You're being intimidated."

Addie grinned. "Don't let Chad bully me," she said.

"Exactly," her father said and kissed the top of her head lightly. "I don't know why I worry about you. You're a smart kid."

The phone rang, and Addie listened as her mother answered. "Addie," her mom called up the stairs. "The phone's for you."

Addie jumped off the bed. "End of discussion?" she asked her father.

He nodded, and she hugged him tightly before she skipped from the room.

"It's probably Nick," she said, running down the stairs. "Can I go riding, Mom?"

But her mother was holding her hand over the receiver. "I think it's Chad," she said in a low voice.

Addie wrinkled her nose and stared at the phone.

"Well, take it," her mother said with a chuckle and held the phone out.

Reluctantly, Addie took the phone. "Hello?"

"Addie. This is Chadwick. Granny asked me to contact you. You don't need to be concerned about food tomorrow. She's going to fix us a picnic lunch."

"Okay," Addie said. "That's nice. Tell her thanks."

"We also need to see one of the wooden figures again. Emily and I still have some questions as to what they are and... and what exactly it is we're looking for and... and..." Chad faltered a little. "So please bring the one with the overalls."

Addie hesitated. "Did your grandmother ask us to bring it?"

"*I'm* asking you to bring it," Chad said.

"Your grandmother wanted to leave them with Mrs. Brady so she could get started on her painting," Addie reminded him.

"Granny won't care."

Addie thought quickly. "Then you'd better have your grandmother call Mrs. Brady so she can send it with Nick in the morning, okay?"

Silence.

"I'll see you tomorrow, Chad," Addie said.

Click.

CHAPTER 10

Visiting Jerome

Nick had cheered up considerably by the time Addie and her father picked him up the next morning. Addie decided not to tell him about her phone conversation with Chad.

It would be nice if we could all start out in good moods this morning, she thought to herself.

Long Pond Road stretched all the way from the south end of Mt. Pilot to the north, and Mrs. Tyler lived at the very end, near the small pond the road was named for. Chad and Emily were waiting for them in a swing on the front porch of a two-story, Victorian-style house. Emily ran out to the car to greet them as they got their bikes from the back.

"This is going to be so much fun!" she exclaimed. "I don't even care if we find anything. At least I won't have to sit around with old stick-in-the-mud Chad for the next two weeks."

Addie glanced up at the porch. Chad was watching them. He seemed to look both Addie and Nick over very carefully, then he frowned. Addie knew he was disappointed that they hadn't brought the wooden figure.

They propped their bikes against the front porch and waved goodbye to Mr. McCormick. Chad hopped out of the swing and ran lightly down the front steps.

"Let's get started," he said without even a hello.

Let's get started, Nick mouthed behind his back and gave Addie a disgusted look.

So much for good moods, Addie thought.

Chad led them all into the backyard. On a patio near the back door was a large, round metal table painted white with a rainbow-striped umbrella through the middle of it. Four white metal chairs were placed around it. A large black notebook sat in the center of the table.

"Here's the journal," Emily said with a sigh. "It wasn't any help at all."

"We have yet to complete our reading, Emily," Chad said in a formal tone. "At this point, I've noted five references to various types of celebrations. Two birthdays, one anniversary, one family reunion, and a funeral."

Nick stared at the other boy. "Only you would think a funeral was a celebration," he said.

"Sidney expressed very little sorrow at the death," Chad told him. "He even said the family was rejoicing because the de...de...decayed person was finished with his suffering and he was home with the Lord."

"I think you mean deceased," Addie said, trying hard to keep the laughter out of her voice. "Sidney must have been a Christian."

Emily gave her a funny look. "So? Who isn't?"

Addie took a deep breath and exchanged a quick glance with Nick. He had one hand up to hide the other and was pointing at Chad. Addie frowned at him.

"We're not here to discuss the Danners' souls," Chad told his sister. "We've got to figure out what celebration the poem refers to, and who Nellie is."

"Has the journal mentioned Nellie?" Nick asked.

Chad shook his head. "There was one mention of a friend named Nelson, but the masculine diminutive of Nelson is Nels, not Nellie."

"Yeah, that's true," Nick murmured. Then his eyes widened in surprise, and he looked at Chad. "Hey, I'm actually beginning to understand you. That's a scary thought."

"Nick," Addie said in a warning voice.

Chad ignored them both. "I'm not sure where to go from here. The only thing I can do is finish reading the rest of the entries." He sat down in one of the metal chairs and began to read.

Addie, Nick, and Emily looked at one another. Nick clasped his hands and began twiddling his thumbs. Addie smacked his arm. "Cut it out," she whispered.

"Well, what are we supposed to do while the master reads?" Nick wanted to to know.

Addie turned to Emily. "Your grandma said there weren't many people who would remember her parents. But there might be one or two. Let's go ask her if she can give us any names."

The three children ran into the kitchen through the back door. A large pan full of freshly baked cinnamon rolls sat on the kitchen table. Emily saw the expression on Nick's face and grinned.

"We can have one for a snack," she said and hurried through the room into the dining room.

Mrs. Tyler's house reminded Addie of Miss T.'s home before she remodeled. All the rooms were large and square and sparsely furnished with worn, comfortable furniture. Mrs. Tyler was sitting at the dining room table, cutting out a pattern for a girl's dress. She smiled at the three children.

"Granny, do you know of anyone who might remember your parents?" Emily asked her grandmother.

Mrs. Taylor sighed. "Oh, dear, there aren't many left. Let me think." She finished cutting out one side of the pattern and put her scissors down. "Martha Danner was Sidney's first cousin—well, by law anyway. She married one of the Danner cousins. But she goes to Florida every year for six months. She doesn't come home until the middle of June. Who else?"

The woman continued talking to herself as she pulled pins out of the pattern and stuck them back in the pincushion. "Of course, Davis Danner could have told you anything you wanted to know, but he died last year. Jerome!"

She smiled triumphantly at the three children. "Jerome Harris was a good friend of my father's. After Sidney and Stella died, Jerome kept in touch with my aunt. He always wanted to know how I was doing in school, sent me cards on holidays, that kind of thing. I'm sure he'd be happy to talk with you."

"Where does he live?" Nick asked.

"The last I heard, Jerome was in Country Manor Retirement Center. He's had a small stroke and can't live alone anymore. But his mind is still fairly clear. Why don't you go visit Jerome?"

Country Manor Retirement Center was on the edge of Mt. Pilot. It had been converted from a private home and was nestled in among a small grove of trees, with lots of flower beds and bushes. It looked like a nice enough place, but none of the children had ever been there.

"What do you mean by 'fairly' clear?" Nick asked.

"Oh, you know how old people are," Mrs. Tyler said cheerfully. "Sometimes they can remember the tiniest detail and other times they forget their own name. I'm sure Jerome could help you, though."

Addie agreed. They didn't have much choice, really. If they wanted to make sense of the latest clue, they needed more help.

"Let's go," she said to the other two, but Emily and Nick both hesitated.

"Are you sure they'll let four kids in there?" Emily asked.

"Oh, of course, dear," said her grandmother. "Old people love to see children. They'll welcome you with open arms."

"That's what I'm afraid of," Nick muttered. "I had to visit my great-uncle in a nursing home once. Everybody wanted to hug me and pat my cheek." He paused. "I'll stay here and keep Chad company," he offered.

"It's not that bad, Nick," Addie scoffed. "Stay here if you want to." She turned to Emily. "Will you come with me?"

Emily took a deep breath. "Sure," she finally said. "We'll just find Mr. Harris and ask him about Nellie and leave, right?"

"Right," Addie said.

In the end, all four children rode their bikes to Country Manor. Chad had read several more pages in the journal and found nothing. Although he was no more anxious to visit the center than Nick was, he decided to go along, "to make sure all possible avenues of discussion are explored," he said.

Still, Addie was the one who led the small group into the home and up the wide set of stairs to the office above. A kind-looking woman wearing an expensive suit greeted them from behind a big oak desk.

"How can I help you?" she asked Addie.

"We'd like to visit Jerome Harris," the young girl told her. The woman—Mrs. Becket was her name—directed them to a room at the back of the house.

They all walked softly through the long, spacious hall.

"What's his room number?" Emily whispered.

"One-oh-two," Addie whispered back.

The house was very quiet and had a distinct medicinal odor to it. One of the side doors opened suddenly, and all four children jumped. A young man in a white uniform, carrying a tray of tiny plastic cups with pills in them, stepped into the hall.

He grinned at the frightened children. "Who are y'all lookin' for?" he asked in a normal voice.

Addie began to breath regularly again. "Jerome Harris," she answered, and the man pointed to the next room.

Addie thanked him and tapped nervously on the wide wooden door. It was partially open.

"You'll have to knock louder than that," the young man called from down the hall. He tapped one ear to indicate Jerome's problem. Addie nodded and knocked harder.

This time the door swung open slightly, and all four children peered curiously into the room. It was a spacious room, with a hospital bed in one corner. The rest of the room looked like a normal bedroom. In fact, it looked like a very attractive, comfortable bedroom. Two walls were lined with shelves that were full of books. Two large spider plants hung from the ceiling. A reclining chair and a floor lamp sat next to a large window that opened onto the backyard, and the view was beautiful. There were shade trees just beginning to leaf out and flower beds full of blooming tulips. A bird bath sat between two of the tallest trees. Jerome Harris was standing by the window, watching a song sparrow splash in and out of the water.

"Mr. Harris," Addie said. "Mr. Harris," she said again, more loudly this time.

The old man turned around slowly and looked at the children, rather blankly, for just a few seconds. Then he smiled and beckoned them into the room.

"Come in, come in," he said in a strong, deep voice. "Have a seat, right here. No, here, don't stand, there's plenty of room for you all. Please sit down, dear."

Once he had settled Addie and Emily on the bed, Nick on the window seat, and Chad in a straight-back chair by the desk, he perched on the edge of his reclining chair and smiled.

"How are you?" he asked jovially.

"Fine," Addie said, and the other children murmured in agreement.

"Who are you?" he asked, just as jovially.

The four children all laughed nervously, then took turns introducing themselves. Even then, it took Addie several minutes of patient explanation before Jerome understood who the children were and why they were there.

"I was with Sidney at the hospital the day he died," the old man murmured sadly. "Cancer, you know. So young, so young." He gave Addie a puzzled look. "He never told me about any scavenger hunt."

"I think it was meant to be something special between him and his brother," Addie told him.

"Oh, yes," Jerome nodded. "Those two boys always had something special between them. They was as close as brothers could be. They was always cookin' up sumpin'. Good friends, they was."

"Did they ever fight?" Nick asked him.

"All the time," Jerome said.

"Good friends don't fight all the time," Chad scoffed.

"Remember now, they was brothers too," Jerome said. "If you had any brothers or sisters, you'd be understandin' that."

Chad and Emily looked at one another, and Emily made a face at her brother. He scowled at her.

"We've been able to figure out the first two clues in the scavenger hunt," Addie told Mr. Harris, "but the third one is really hard. We thought maybe someone who knew Mr. Danner might be able to help us."

"Well, where is this clue?" Jerome asked her.

They all looked at one another. No one had remembered to bring the clue with them.

"I think I've got it memorized," Addie said. She thought for a few moments, then closed her eyes and repeated the verse. "'We raise our voice in celebration, in a style so free and grand, when we celebrate our nation, even Nellie takes a stand.'"

Jerome listened intently, one hand cupped behind his ear to help him hear better. When Addie finished, he continued to stare at her as he sat back in his reclining chair.

Suddenly his face crinkled into hundreds of tiny lines, and he smiled hugely. Then he began to laugh.

He laughed and laughed, and the children began to look at one another with worried glances. Finally

Mr. Harris sat up and pulled a white handkerchief from his back pocket. He wiped his eyes and took a deep breath.

"Nellie," he said. There was still a chuckle in his voice. "Oh, my. I haven't thought of Nellie for years and years. Now there's a story!"

CHAPTER 11

Nellie

The old man sat back in his chair and a faraway look came into his eyes. He smiled gently and seemed to forget the children were there. Finally Nick spoke.

"Could you tell us about Nellie?" he asked.

The sound of his voice made the old man jump, and he looked at them all with surprise. "Oh, yes," he said. "Of course. You wanted to know about Nellie."

He folded his handkerchief into a perfect square and put it back in his pocket. "Isn't much to tell, really. Just one of those boyhood pranks. Brings back lots of memories, though.

"We was right in the middle of the Great Depression. Being kids, we didn't let it put a worry on us. We knew we didn't have no money to buy fun, so we made our own fun. One afternoon, about two weeks before Independence Day, we noticed some fellas in the park, working on the statue of Nellie Graff.

"Nellie was a statue the Ladies Aide Society erected after World War One. Nellie was a nurse from Mt. Pilot who died on the battlefield. Everyone was real proud 'a her.

"But Nellie was showing some wear and tear, so these fellas had her down off her pedestal, shinin' her up. Well, bein' a Friday afternoon, I guess they thought they could take off work a mite early. They left Nellie sittin' on this little platform.

"Me and Sid and Frank and some other fellas saw these guys leave. Of course, we couldn't resist goin' over to examine Nellie up close. There were still folks goin' in and out of the park, but nobody paid much mind to us. I guess they thought Nellie was too heavy to move, so nobody worried about her."

Jerome began to laugh again, and his whole body shook. He took his handkerchief out to wipe his eyes. Finally he continued.

"She *was* heavy, but there was six 'a us and only one 'a her. And when we all got our hands up under the base—remember she was on a platform—we discovered she was hollow. Well, that opened up all sorts of possibilities!

"We tipped Nellie over just enough so one of us could fit up inside her. We elected Sid, 'cause he was the smallest *and* he had the best singing voice.

"Once Sid got inside, we set Nellie back up and then we all kinda spread out around the park and watched. Whenever somebody would walk by the statue, Sid would wait until he thought they was real close, then he'd burst out singin' 'The Star Spangled Banner.'"

Jerome was chuckling again, and now all the children were laughing with him. "Oh, I wish you could have seen some 'a those ladies jump! Sid stayed in there for a while, then we decided we all wanted turns. So we'd wait till no one was around, tip her over, and switch places.

"Frank was the last one to take his turn, and just as we got him settled inside, who should walk up but Officer Reynolds. Wanted to know what we was doing. 'Course, in those days, a policeman could put the fear in a bunch of young boys. None 'a us was goin' to admit what we'd been up to, so he chased us out 'a the park. Told us not to come back, he'd be watchin' for us."

Now the children were quiet, all eyes on Jerome. "He was true to his word. Patrolled around that park the rest 'a the night. Every once in a while, Sid would sneak by the statue to let Frank know we hadn't abandoned him.

"But it got late, and the rest of us had to go home for supper. So we made a vow to sneak back that night at ten o'clock to let Frank out. Officer Reynolds always went home at nine-thirty.

"Sid was the only one who didn't leave. Stayed in the park, talkin' to Frank when Reynolds wasn't looking. I tell you, that was one long night for poor Frank. But we got back at ten, tipped ol' Nellie on her side, and got Frank out." Jerome shook his head. "He sure was one hot, sweaty kid."

"Did you ever tell anyone about it?" Addie asked.

"Did your parents ever find out?" was Nick's question.

"Whole town found out about it," Jerome answered, "including our parents. Officer Reynolds knew Frank was in there. Figured it'd teach us all a lesson if we had to leave him there for a couple 'a hours."

The old man smiled to himself and shook his head slowly. "He was right," was all he said.

"So do you think Sid hid the next package inside Nellie?" Emily asked in excitement. "If he did, all we have to do is go to the park and get inside the statue!"

"And just how to you propose to do that?" Chad asked his sister.

"We could lift the statue too," she said.

"There's only four of us, and two of us are girls," Chad said disdainfully.

Addie let that one pass. "We'd have to get someone from the park district to help us. If Nellie's back on her pedestal, she's attached permanently."

Jerome was shaking his head. "They moved Nellie after World War II. Put up a new statue for all the fallen soldiers in both wars."

"Where is she now?" Emily asked.

"Last I heard," Jerome said, "she was in that little gazebo they put up a few years back in Westside Park."

"Let's go!" Emily said, jumping off the bed.

Chad stood up too, but Nick and Addie just looked at one another.

"What's the matter?" Emily asked.

"That park was destroyed in the tornado," Addie said. "The gazebo's not there anymore."

Emily sank back to the bed, but Chad stayed where he was, a frown on his face. "It's a statue, for heaven's sake," he said impatiently. "It couldn't have been destroyed. Even if the gazebo's gone, they probably saved the statue."

"Have you ever been in a tornado?" Nick asked him bluntly.

Chad shook his head.

"Then don't think you know what it can and can't do," Nick told him. "This whole search started because Addie and I found that pickup truck on its side in the creek. If a tornado can flip a truck an eighth of a mile, it can take out a statue."

For once Chad didn't have a comeback. Emily did.

"We won't know unless we look," she said. "Have you been to the park since the tornado? Are you absolutely sure the statue's gone?"

Addie shook her head. "No. We've driven by several times. To be honest, I never noticed the statue when the gazebo was standing, so I never looked to see if it was gone." She jumped off the bed.

"Emmie's right," she said. "Let's go look."

Jerome eased himself out of his reclining chair. "Well, good luck to you," he said, and Addie reached out to pat his arm.

"Thanks," she said. "That was a wonderful story."

"It was a wonderful time," Jerome said quietly.

"We'll come back and tell you if we find anything," Nick said.

Jerome smiled. "You can come back, even if you don't find anything."

With a promise to return, the four children left the retirement home and rode slowly towards the other side of town.

"We need to check in with Granny," Emmie said. "We've been gone more than an hour. She'll worry if she doesn't know where we're at."

Mrs. Tyler was watching out the window for the children, and she motioned them inside. "I've got cinnamon rolls and milk ready if you want a snack," she told them.

Between the four of them, they managed to eat about two-thirds of the pan of rolls and several glasses of milk. Mrs. Tyler watched them with a smile on her face. "You won't want any of the lunch I've packed for you," she laughed.

"Sure we will," Nick told her. "We're riding out to Westside Park. By the time we get there, we'll be famished."

"What's at Westside Park?" Mrs. Tyler asked.

Emmie told her grandmother the story of the "singing statue" and Mrs. Tyler laughed until tears came to her eyes. "Oh, this is wonderful," she said. "I'm learning more about my father in these few days than I've known all my life. I'm so glad you're working together on this."

Lunch in hand, the children left shortly afterwards, and Nick led the way across town to the small park located in the southwest corner of the village.

Westside Park was a dismal sight, and the four children rode silently down the gravel drive that wound through the playground and back to the gazebo. There were no swing sets or teeter-totters left. Only the slide remained, and it was twisted so that it lifted up off the ground. If you tried to slide down it, you'd have to jump off the end.

The gazebo was indeed gone. The foundation was still standing, and the short white picket fence that had been erected to cover the bare concrete was missing boards and lying flat on the ground in some places.

Members of the park district had been working to clean up the damage caused by the tornado. There was a huge stack of lumber and shingles next to the spot where the gazebo had been.

Nick jumped up onto the bare foundation, and Addie followed him. In the middle of the stage, there was a huge hole. Nick peered into it.

"This is where she was," he said. Chad and Emmie joined them, and they all studied the hole. Then Nick dropped down into it. "Let's make sure the package didn't fall in here," he said.

The hole was bigger than any of them realized. Nick dropped to his knees and crawled out of their sight. "Hey, I can crawl all the way under here," he called out to them, and his voice echoed oddly inside the concrete foundation. He reappeared quickly. "But it's too dark to see anything."

Addie pulled her father's flashlight from the back pocket of her jeans and handed it to Nick. Everyone stared at her.

"Always be prepared," she said and grinned at Nick.

He took the flashlight and crawled away once more.

"Can't we go too?" Emmie wanted to know.

Nick heard her question and yelled back to them. "You could come down here, but there's nothing much to see. A bunch of dirt and a bunch of garbage and a—hey!"

All of a sudden the other three children heard a scraping sound and in a matter of seconds, Nick appeared outside the foundation, on the other side.

"There's a door under here," he said. "If Nellie was still here, we could have gotten under the foundation and inside the statue with no problem."

"If the statue was still here," Chad said glumly.

Nick brushed the dirt from his knees. "So what do we do now?" he asked, returning Addie's flashlight.

Addie turned in a slow circle, looking the park over carefully to make sure the statue had not been salvaged and moved somewhere else. She saw nothing but a wheelbarrow parked beside a small storage shed.

Everyone followed her gaze.

"It's probably just a tool shed," Chad said.

"And it's probably locked," Nick said.

"But..." Emmie began.

"We won't know until we try," they all finished for her and took off running.

The shed had a padlock on the latch, and Nick pulled at it in frustration. It opened in his hand. He looked at the other three children.

"Nick..." Chad began and Nick grinned.

"Don't lecture me," he said. "That's Addie's job."

"We'll just look inside," Addie told Chad. "If there's nothing but tools, we'll put the padlock back on and leave." Nick took the padlock off the latch and opened the door.

The shed was dark inside, and they could feel hot air drift out of the open door. Addie swung the beam of the flashlight in a slow arc around the inside. There were rakes, shovels, handsaws, chainsaws, hedge trimmers, and a statue.

Laying on her side and taking up almost half of the shed was Nellie Graff. Emmie squealed in excitement, and all four children crowded inside.

If the statue was a true representation, Nellie had been a small woman with a kind face and a big nose. She was dented in several places, and her whole surface was an odd shade of green. The base of the statue was jagged. It was obvious the tornado had torn Nellie from her stand and tossed her around.

"Who wants to crawl inside and look for the package?" Nick asked.

Neither Addie nor Emmie volunteered. Chad shifted uncomfortably from one foot to the other.

"Okay, I'll go," Nick said. He dropped to the ground and peered inside. "Give me the flashlight," he ordered.

Addie gave it to him, and Nick got onto his stomach and slithered into the hollow statue. He wriggled inside until only his ankles and shoes were showing. Then he gave a shout.

"Here it is!" he yelled, and Emily practically screamed in excitement. They heard a ripping sound. "I've got it. It was taped to her nose."

Nick's feet and legs began to emerge, then he stopped. "Wait a minute," he said from inside the belly of the statue. "I've just got to do this."

Addie, Emily, and Chad all looked at one another. They could hear Nick clear his throat, and then he began to sing.

"Oh-oh, say, can you see . . ."

CHAPTER 12

Frank Danner

Even Chad grinned as they listened to Nick's changing voice waver through the final strains of "The Star Spangled Banner." Addie held her breath, waiting for the high note on "the land of the free." He'd squeaked his way through "the rocket's red glare." It didn't sound as if he had much breath left.

But Nick fooled them all and dropped an octave when he came to "Oh, say, does that star-spangled banner yet wave." He finished the song in a slightly off-key but heartfelt bass, and Addie and Emily began applauding before the final note faded away.

Nick slid the rest of the way out and handed the

package to Emily. She grabbed it willingly and slipped out of the shed and into the sunlight. The others followed her.

"How did that sound?" Nick asked.

"Don't quit your day job," Chad muttered with a grin.

Nick gave an exaggerated bow to an imaginary audience. "Thank you, thank you," he said.

Emily was pulling at the seams of the oilskin package. "I can't get this open!" she cried in frustration.

Addie shook her head. "You have to cut it open. You can't tear it with your hands."

"Calm down, Emmie," Chad said, but he said it with patience, and Addie and Nick exchanged a surprised glance. "There are plenty of tools in here. We'll just use the hedge trimmers to cut it open."

He stepped back inside the shed and returned with a small pair of trimmers. He took the package and snipped into it with ease. Emily couldn't contain her excitement.

"Let me see, let me see," she demanded, and Chad gave her the package with a frown.

Just then, a voice behind them said, "What's going on here?"

All four children jumped. A tall woman in khaki shorts and an olive drab tee shirt stood behind them. She had dark blond hair plaited in a braid that hung to her waist, and her eyes were large and bright green.

"I said, what's going on?"

Chad spoke first. "We were looking for the statue of Nellie Graff."

"Why?" the woman asked.

Emily held up her package, and the woman frowned. "What's that?"

Addie began to explain the purpose of their visit, but Nick interrupted her. "Who are you?" he asked.

The woman looked Nick over and smiled. "Fair question." She tapped an identification badge that was clipped to the bottom of her shirt. "My name is Amanda Gaffner," she said. "I work with the park district. We've had some problems with vandals in the last few days, so I'm naturally suspicious. Who are you?"

This time Nick let Addie give the woman a brief summary of their search, and Amanda listened with interest. By the time Addie got to the part about the "singing statue" and their search for Nellie, Emily had opened the package and freed the little wooden figure from his fifty-year confinement. She held him up for everyone to see.

This figure was even more elaborate than the first two. His eyes were tiny blue rhinestones that had lost their sparkle, and his smile had been painted, not carved. His clothes were painted on front and back. He had a dark blue bandanna around his neck, with a blue-and-red plaid shirt and blue pants. Boots had been painted on his feet, with the toes pointing out. There were white rhinestone buttons on his shirt and one on each of his boots.

"It's a cowboy," Emmie exclaimed.

After all the children had examined the little man, Amanda asked to look at him. She turned the figure over in her hand.

"It's a miracle you ever found this," she told the children. "Nellie was in storage for decades. In fact, the village was going to junk her about five years ago. But some old guy donated the money to have her restored and set up here at Westside.

"When the tornado took her down, we decided it would be best to get rid of her for good. We were keeping her in the shed until we could get a truck out here to haul her away."

Nick caught Addie's eye and looked heavenward. *Thank You, Lord!* he mouthed, and Addie grinned.

"Who donated the money to have her restored?" Emily asked.

"I don't know," Amanda said. "I think it's on the plaque."

"Can we look?" Addie asked. She had a feeling she knew who the man was.

"Sure, go ahead." Amanda nodded toward the shed, and Addie flicked on her flashlight and stepped inside to examine the statue.

She found the plaque near the jagged edge of the base. Its inscription was simple. *In memory. FJD*

"Just what I thought," Addie told the others. "Frank Danner."

Amanda Gaffner took the trimmers from Chad and put them back in the shed. "Anything else you need?" she asked.

"No," Nick told her. "This is what we came for."

"Next time," Amanda said in a friendly voice, "try to get permission before you go snooping around government property." She shut the door to the shed and snapped the padlock closed.

They got back on their bikes and waved to Amanda as they rode out of the park. Once they were out of earshot, Nick began to grumble.

"I thought parks were public property," he said.

"Public parks are maintained by tax dollars," Chad began, "and as such are under the jurisdiction of—"

"Can it, Chad," Emily said. "I'm hungry. Who's got the lunches?"

Addie held up the large brown bag Mrs. Tyler had packed. "Let's find someplace to eat this," she said. "I'm anxious to read the next clue."

Emily's eyes widened. "I forgot about the clue!" she cried and tried to peer inside the oilskin bag and steer her bike at the same time.

"Don't open the bag, Emmie," Chad said sharply. "The clue might blow out in this wind."

Emily clamped the bag shut with her hand, but she stood up to ride. "Hurry!" she called over her shoulder. "Let's eat at the town square. It's right up here. Come on!"

The other three had to stand up and pedal just to keep up with her. Chad pulled ahead and caught up with his sister, but Nick and Addie stayed behind.

"Those two are like Jekyll and Hyde," Nick said to Addie in a low voice. "Chad won't hardly crack a smile, and Emily goes into a frenzy over every little thing."

Addie just smiled. "I'm beginning to like them," she told him. "Especially Emily."

Nick frowned. "Yeah, me too," he admitted. "And Chad actually reverted into English there for a little while. Did you notice?"

Addie laughed, but she didn't bother to answer. She picked up speed and followed Emily and Chad into the main park in the center of Mt. Pilot. Emily had already dropped her bike at the nearest picnic table and was digging in the oilskin bag for the next clue.

She found it and was waving it in Chad's face but snatched it away when he tried to take it from her.

"Come on, Emmie," he demanded. "I let you see the cowboy first. I should get to read the clue."

Emily gave up the clue with reluctance, and Chad read the words, his lips moving silently.

Addie plunked the lunch bag down on the table and opened it up. She pulled out four sandwiches and a large bag of chips. There were also several apples and bananas in the bottom of the bag, along with boxed fruit juice and a half-pound bag of M&Ms.

"Read it out loud, Chad." Emily gave her brother a poke in the ribs, and he elbowed her away.

"All right, all right," he said.

> Hidden away, hot and high,
> Where the flies buzz and the dust flies,
> We take a chance, with a shout and a leap,
> And hope we land all in one piece.

Chad just shook his head and handed the note to his sister. She read it and passed it to Addie. Addie munched on her sandwich and looked the clue over carefully before giving it to Nick.

"Sounds like they're going to jump off of something," he said.

Emily giggled. "No kidding," she said. "I think we all figured out that part."

"But what are they jumping off of, and where is it at?" Chad asked.

"It's up high, and it's hidden," Addie said between bites.

"And it's hot," Emily added.

"Maybe a bridge?" Nick crunched into an apple and juice sprayed across the table.

"Thanks a lot," Emily said and wiped the side of her face.

Addie shook her head. "A bridge isn't really hidden. And besides, we've already found one clue under a bridge—kind of. I don't think he'd use the same place twice."

"It's got to be some place where flies buzz and dust flies," Chad said. He tossed a peanut M&M high in the air and caught it expertly in his mouth.

"Eat your sandwich first, Chad," Emily commanded.

Chad ignored her and continued catching M&Ms. Nick joined him, but his average was poor and more M&Ms ended up in the grass than in his mouth. Chad finally moved the bag where Nick couldn't reach it.

"You're wasting them," he said.

Nick made a face and went back to his sandwich. "What about a tree?" he asked suddenly. "You can get high up in a tree and still be hidden. And if it's summertime, flies buzz around you."

"That's a possibility," Addie said.

"Trees aren't very permanent," Emily argued. "I don't think Sidney would hide a clue some place that might not last for a long time."

Addie looked at the younger girl. "That's a good point," she said. "He knew the root cellar and the bridge and the statue would be there for a long time."

"The statue wasn't," Nick pointed out.

"But that's not something Sidney could have foreseen," Addie said. "According to Jerome, the whole town made a big fuss over Nellie's statue. Sidney probably thought it would be there forever."

Addie opened one of the boxes of fruit juice and jabbed the straw through the pre-punched hole. She sipped at her drink, and everyone else munched in silence on sandwiches and fruit.

A long, black car pulled into the gravel parking lot under the shade trees on the other side of the park. Addie watched an older man in a short-sleeve shirt and dark pants step out of the car. He locked the door and slipped the keys in his pocket.

"Give me some M&Ms, Chad," Emily commanded, and Chad passed the half-empty bag across the table. Emily frowned. "Addie and I get the rest of these," she said.

"What about me?" Nick asked.

"Get yours out of the grass," Emily said with a grin, but she passed the bag to Nick and he took a handful.

"I still think I can do this," he murmured and tossed an M&M high into the air. He had to lean back to catch it, and it bonked him on the nose and flew off into the grass.

Chad snorted, and Nick took another piece of candy. "One more time," he said.

He threw it high and leaned back. This time he caught it and almost choked, then lost his balance and fell off the bench backwards onto the ground. Everyone else shouted with laughter. No one noticed the man until he was at their table.

Emily gave a little gasp at his sudden appearance, and he frowned. "Are you one of the Tyler children?" he asked.

Emily nodded.

"And you're the McCormick girl?"

Addie nodded.

"My name is Frank Danner. I want to talk to all of you."

CHAPTER 13

Off Limits

Frank Danner was a thin man of medium build. He wasn't tall, and he wasn't short, just somewhere in between. His arms and face were tanned a permanent, mottled-brown color that old farmers all shared. His hairline had slipped past the halfway point on his head. What hair he had left was pure white, as were his eyebrows. But his eyes were dark, almost black, and they seemed to cut right through Addie.

"Ron Kleiss says you've been snooping around my property. Why?" he wanted to know.

"We . . . we found some things," Addie stammered.

"You're trespassing on private property, and I want it to stop." He said the words without anger, but there was no doubt in any of the children's minds he meant what he said.

Nick tried to reason with him. "I think you'd be interested in what we've found," he began.

"Then you'd better think again," the old man said rudely. "I don't care what you've found, and I don't care what you do with it. Just stay off my property from now on."

He turned on his heel and strode away. The four children watched in stunned silence. Then Emily jumped up and stamped her foot on the ground.

"Wait just a minute!" She shouted the words at the old man's back, and Addie, Nick, and Chad turned to stare at her.

Mr. Danner turned as well, slowly, and he fixed the young girl with a piercing gaze. Emily faltered, but she didn't back down.

"I . . . I'm your niece, and I don't think that was very . . . very polite," she said in a more subdued voice. "We're family."

When her uncle simply continued to stare at her, she hurried on. "We've found clues to a scavenger hunt that your brother Sidney set up for *you*," she told Frank. "The first three clues led to three little wooden men. We found the fourth clue today."

Frank gazed at her for another long moment, then held out his hand.

Emily snatched the paper from the top of the picnic table and ran to her great-uncle. She handed him the paper, chattering excitedly. "Addie and Nick found the first two little men, and today we found the third one with the next clue—"

She stopped abruptly. Mr. Danner was still staring at her. He crumpled the paper in his fist, then shook his fist slowly in Emily's face.

"Stay off my property," he said and left.

They watched in silence until Frank Danner's car backed out of the lot and sped away. Emily returned to the group, blinking furiously to keep back the tears. She sat down and propped her elbows on the table. She covered her eyes with fists clenched so tightly her knuckles were white.

"Aw, come on, Emmie," Chad said awkwardly. "Don't let that old coot get to you."

Emily took a deep, jagged breath. "That old *coot* has our clue."

"What difference does it make?" Addie asked quietly. "There's nothing we can do about it now."

Emily rubbed the last of her tears away and looked at Addie in disbelief. "You're not going to quit, are you?"

It was Addie's turn to be surprised. "You heard what he said, Emmie. We can't go back on his property."

"So?" Chad joined his sister. "He's never there. How will he know?"

Nick and Addie exchanged an uneasy glance. "We have to respect his wishes," Nick finally said. "If he doesn't—"

"This is important to me and Emmie—and it's important to Granny!" Chad interrupted.

"I don't think she'd want you to trespass if your uncle told you not to," Addie said.

"I don't care," Chad said stubbornly.

"Me neither," Emmie said. "Those toys belonged to our great-grandfather, and we want to find them. And that old booger's not going to stop us!"

Chad crammed the empty chip bag, the plastic sandwich bags, and all the empty fruit juice boxes into the brown paper sack. He tossed the nearly-empty bag of M&Ms at Nick. "Like I said before, we don't need you guys."

He shoved the whole sackful of garbage in a nearby trash can. Then he picked up the bag with the little wooden man. He got on his bike and rode away, with Emily right behind him.

Addie watched them until they disappeared from view. She made no move to go after them, and neither did Nick. Finally he spoke.

"Great. Now what do we do?"

Addie didn't have an answer. Nick turned the M&M bag upside down and three peanut candies rolled out onto the picnic table. He leaned over and sucked the closest one into his mouth.

"Nick!" Addie shuddered. "You do some of the grossest things."

"Oh, I'm sorry. Did you want one?" he asked politely. He sucked in the second one and rolled the third one across the table to Addie.

"Yuk." She rolled it back. Nick lined himself up and let it roll off the table and into his mouth. Addie didn't even smile.

They got on their bikes and rode slowly out of the park. There was traffic at the corner so Nick leaned against the curb and waited for it to pass.

Addie sighed. "It's so frustrating. There's still one little man left to find, and we can't do a thing about it."

"Even if we wanted to, we don't have the clue," Nick reminded her.

"'Hidden away, hot and high, where the flies buzz and the dust flies, we take a chance, with a shout and leap, and hope we land all in one piece.'" Addie repeated the verse from memory.

Nick stared at her, and his eyes lit up. "So we could do something about it."

Addie just looked at him.

"If we wanted to, that is," he said. "Which we don't." Pause. "Do we?"

"We want to, we just can't."

"Yeah, I know," he said with a sigh. "But it makes me mad. We did most of the work. And now Chad and Emily are going to have all the fun. *They're* not going to stop looking."

Addie nodded. Was this the way God was going to answer her prayer? She'd tried to compromise with Chad and Emily. And she thought she was doing a pretty good job. But now they seemed to be at a dead end. *So what's the point, Lord?*

There was no clap of thunder or lightning bolt for an answer. Addie shook her head and tried to put it out of her mind. "We're supposed to meet your mom at Mrs. Tyler's," she said to Nick, "but I don't feel like going back there. Which doctor does Jesse go to? Maybe we can catch her at the office."

They found the Bradys' van parked outside Dr. Warner's office. Addie and Nick were loading their bikes in the back just as Mrs. Brady came out of the front door with Jesse Kate in tow. The little girl was crying softly and hiccupping loudly. When she saw Nick and Addie, she burst into fresh tears.

"Yeah, I know how you feel," Nick murmured and took his sister from his mother's arms.

"Shots," Mrs. Brady explained. "So how did you do this morning? Did you find anything?"

Nick gave his mother a brief rundown of their morning. He told of their meeting with Jerome Harris and the story of the "singing statue." He ended with their encounter with Frank Danner and the subsequent argument with Chad and Emily.

Mrs. Brady was disappointed. "I'm so sorry it had to turn out this way. I wonder if Mrs. Tyler will want to include the cowboy in her painting? I wonder if she still wants a painting? I'll have to give her a call."

Nick helped Addie get her bike out of the van at the McCormicks' house.

"Thanks, Nick," she said. "I'll call you tomorrow. I think Ron Kleiss is going to pull that truck out of the creek in the morning. Maybe we can watch."

She waved goodbye and walked slowly into the house. Her mother was outside hanging towels on the clothesline, and Addie called to her from the back door. Mrs. McCormick had several clothespins in her mouth, so she simply waved back. Addie went up to her room and spent the rest of the afternoon reading a mystery novel.

Her father came home early for supper, and the three of them grilled hamburgers and hot dogs in the backyard. While they worked, Addie began telling her parents about the events of the day. Mr. McCormick got quite a chuckle out of the "singing statue."

"Sounds like a stunt Nick would pull," he said.

"He did." Addie grinned and told them how they found the cowboy. Then she described their meeting with Frank Danner.

Mr. McCormick handed her a plateful of slightly overdone hamburgers. "You know what that means, don't you?" he asked.

Addie carried the plate to the picnic table. She nodded. "Yeah. We can't go back to the Danner property."

"Except to get my flashlight," Mr. McCormick reminded her. "Is it still in the root cellar?"

Addie nodded.

"What about Chad and Emily?" her father asked.

Addie hesitated. "I think they're going to keep looking," she said.

Mr. McCormick frowned. "Somehow, that doesn't surprise me. But it is their great-grandfather. I can understand their curiosity."

"I'm curious too," Addie murmured.

"I know you are, kiddo," her father said sympathetically, "and I'm sorry it turned out this way. But—" He paused and smiled. "I think this is part of the lesson the Lord's teaching you about compromise."

"What do you mean?"

"First, the Lord showed you that you needed to learn to compromise," her father said. "Then He gave you some practice with Chad and Emily. Now you're learning the flip side—when *not* to compromise."

"That's the hardest part," Addie grumbled. "I don't mind doing what's right if I know why I'm doing it. It would be easier if Mr. Danner had a reason to keep us off his property. But he doesn't." Addie could hear the whine in her voice, but she didn't care.

Her father did. "He doesn't need a reason," he said firmly. "It's his property, and he makes the rules. You obey the rules, whether or not Chad and Emily do."

When Addie didn't answer, her father tipped her head back so he could look her in the eye. "It's an important lesson to learn, Addie," he insisted. "You won't always know why God asks you to do certain things. You still have to be obedient."

"Okay." Addie tried to smile, and her father gave her a hug.

I had a feeling this was going to be a tough one, Lord. I was right. She finished her meal in silence.

* * *

Addie slept late the next morning. She rode her bike to Nick's house around ten o'clock. When she knocked on the screen door, Jesse Kate came running from the far end of the house. The little girl stood and waved at Addie from the door of the kitchen. Then Nick appeared and opened the screen.

"You're late," he said. "I've already been down to the creek. Mr. Kleiss has the truck up on one end. They were switching the chains around to pull it out, so I came home to change my shoes and get my camera. We'll have to hurry."

Nick was taking off his good Nikes as he talked. He pulled on a pair of grungy old sneakers and tried to tie the laces. While he tied the right one, Jesse untied the left, and he scolded her gently. "Stop it, Jess," he said. "I'm in a hurry."

Addie picked up the little girl and spun her in a circle to distract her. Jesse squealed and thumped Nick on the head with Mr. Nose when they spun past him.

"Ouch. I'm leaving again, Mom! I'll be home by lunchtime."

"Have fun, dear," Mrs. Brady answered from the kitchen.

Addie gave Jesse a quick kiss and set her down. Jesse was still a little dizzy, and she waved a tottery goodbye as the two older children ran out the front door.

By the time they got back to the creek, Mr. Kleiss and a friend had the chains switched. They were pulling the truck up the steep embankment. Water gushed from the cab, and Nick slid down to the water's edge, snapping pictures as he went.

The truck was still dripping water as they pulled it over the top of the embankment and into the field. Then Mr. Kleiss switched the chains once more, and Addie and Nick watched him tow the truck through the field to the road.

"Well, that was pretty cool," Nick said. "And I got a lot of good pictures."

Addie nodded. With the removal of the truck, the water in the drainage ditch flowed freely once more. It was amazing to see how quickly the brush and debris cleared out. Some of it was still caught along the banks, but Addie could tell the creek would soon be clean again.

She looked south across the field to the Danner property. The old barn was a distant speck. Nick followed her gaze.

"Did you get orders to stay away too?" he asked.

Addie nodded. "We have to get Dad's flashlight. After that, it's off limits."

"Why don't we walk over there now?" Nick asked. "It's closer if we cut through the field. We can walk back and get our bikes later."

"Okay."

They set off through the freshly plowed dirt. In a manner of minutes they were on the Danner property. They walked past the demolished house to the root cellar in the back of the huge yard.

Together they lifted the old wooden door, and Addie pulled the large flashlight from her pocket. She went down the steps first, and Nick followed.

"Where'd you leave it?" she asked him.

"I tossed it on the floor when I started to pull out those bricks," he said. "It must have rolled into that corner."

Addie swung the beam of her flashlight into the corner closest to the door, and there was the flashlight. Nick retrieved it, and they both headed back up the short flight of steps. Addie stopped suddenly, and Nick bumped into her.

She turned to him and put a finger to her lips. "Listen," she mouthed. A young girl's voice carried across the yard.

"I don't even know where we should begin, Chad," she said. "Besides, I want to see the root cellar first."

"Just be patient, Emmie," Chad answered. "We've got to hide our bikes so no one sees us from the road. Come on, let's put them in the barn. Then we'll start our search."

CHAPTER 14

The Rescue

Nick waited a few moments, then stepped around Addie and cautiously poked his head just above ground level. There was no one in sight. He turned and pulled Addie back down the steps into the cellar. She bumped her head on the low door.

"Ouch," she whispered.

"Oh, be quiet," Nick whispered back. "How in the world did they get out here?"

"I can't believe they rode their bikes all the way from Mt. Pilot," Addie said. "That's over ten miles."

"Whisper!" Nick hissed. "They're going to hear us."

"So what?" Addie whispered back. "Emily wants to see the root cellar and they know where it's at, because we told them. They'll be here any minute. We'll scare them to death if we don't let them know we're down here."

Nick didn't answer, and Addie began to laugh. "Nick, that's cruel!"

"It's the only fun we're going to get out of all of this," he argued. "Come on, let's get out of the light, back here by the far wall." He stopped and listened. "Hurry up, they're coming!"

They stepped to the back of the root cellar, out of the light coming in through the door, and plastered themselves to the cool brick wall.

"Those guys didn't even bother to shut the cellar door," they heard Chad say in a disgusted tone of voice. "Well, come on, Emmie, here it is."

"You go first," Emily said. "There might be a skunk or something down there."

"Hey, I'm not the one who wants to see the root cellar," Chad told her. "If you want to see it, you go first."

"Then I don't want to see it," Emily said.

"Oh, brother," Chad muttered. "All right, I'll go."

Chad trotted down the steps with Emily hanging onto his shirttail. Before their eyes had time to adjust to the darkness, Nick sprang from the back wall with a roar.

"AAAAARRRRRGGGGGGHHHHH!"

Emily gave such an earsplitting scream that Addie had to cover her ears. But the scream died away quickly because Emily was gone.

Chad backed up and smacked his head on the door. Then he peered into the darkness when he heard Nick's laughter. "Emmie, come on back," he called sharply.

He ran up the steps to calm his sister, and Nick and Addie followed. Nick was holding his sides with laughter, but Addie was sober. She could tell they had frightened Emily badly.

"Emmie, we're sorry," she said immediately, before Nick had a chance to speak. "It seemed like a good joke, but it wasn't. We're really sorry."

Addie poked Nick and he nodded. "Yeah," he said, choking back his laughter. "We're sorry."

Even Chad was trying to hide a grin. "Aw, come on, Emmie. You would have done the same thing if you had the chance."

Emmie swallowed hard. Her bottom lip was still trembling, but she managed a grudging smile. "Yeah, I would have," she agreed. She took a deep breath and put her hand on her chest. "My heart is still doing flip-flops."

Suddenly Chad frowned. "Say, what are you guys doing here? I thought you said we had to respect Frank's wishes and all that garbage."

Nick held up the small flashlight. "This belongs to Addie's dad. I left it here when we were looking for the first man."

"Dad said we could come back to get the flashlight. But now we have to leave," Addie finished.

"How did you get here?" Nick wanted to know. "You didn't ride all the way from Mt. Pilot."

Chad shook his head. "No, we didn't. Granny called your house this morning. She wants to put the cowboy in the painting, so she brought him out to your mom. Your mom told her to bring our bikes, and we could all go riding together. But you were gone when we got to your house, so we told Granny we were going to look for you."

"Oh," Nick said.

The four children stared at one another for a few moments, then Addie turned to Nick. "We have to go."

"Yeah."

"Wait," Emmie said. "Could you at least show us where you found the first man, behind the bricks in the cellar? That would be okay with your dad, wouldn't it?"

Addie thought for a moment, then nodded. "I think so. Come on."

They all trooped back into the root cellar, and Addie shone the light on the bricks while Nick pulled them out. Emily and Chad both reached back into the wall out of curiosity.

"That is so cool," Emmie said. "I wish we could have been here when you found it."

Nick began to replace the bricks, but Addie stopped him. "Wait, Nick. Be quiet for a minute."

They listened, and the sound of a car door slamming made them all freeze. Emmie's eyes grew wide with fright.

"Don't freak, Emmie," Chad commanded in a hoarse whisper. "Maybe it's just Granny."

Nick slipped back up the stairs and poked his head above ground level once more. Then he dropped and scrambled back down the stairs.

"Frank Danner!" he hissed.

Emmie gasped out loud, and Chad covered her mouth with his hand. "Quiet!" he told her.

Addie could feel her heart begin to pound. "What are we going to do?" she asked Nick.

"He's going into the barn," Nick told them. "Where did you put your bikes?"

"Inside the last stall," Chad said. "If he doesn't go all the way to the back of the barn, he won't see them."

Chad slipped up the stairs this time. "I don't see him anywhere," he said when he rejoined his friends. "He must be looking around the barn. He's going to find our bikes for sure."

"Why is he out here?" Addie wondered. "He must be looking for the next little man." Then she gasped. "Of course! 'Hidden away, hot and high, where the flies buzz and the dust flies—'"

"'We take a chance, with a shout and a leap, and hope we land all in one piece,'" Chad finished.

"The hayloft!" Nick moaned.

Emily gritted her teeth in frustration. "He's going to find the last man, and the scavenger hunt will be over! It's not fair."

"It was supposed to be his hunt in the first place," Chad reminded her.

"I know," Emily said, "but he doesn't even care about it. We do!"

"He must care or he wouldn't be here," Addie said thoughtfully. "I wish we could see what he's doing."

Nick tiptoed back up the stairs. Still no sign of Frank Danner. He started back down, then stopped and cocked his head to one side to listen. He motioned to the other three children.

They joined him on the steps. There was a scraping sound coming from the barn and someone was talking, but the words weren't audible. Then came a yell.

"Help! Oh, Lord, help me. Help!"

The children froze and stared at one another.

"Do you think it's a trick?" Emmie whispered.

A loud crash followed, and then they heard an unmistakable shout of fear. *"Help!"*

All four children scrambled out of the root cellar and ran across the yard into the barn. They could see Frank Danner from the waist down. He was dangling from the floor of the hayloft, holding himself up by his forearms and elbows. The ladder that had been propped against the wall had crashed to the floor. The second rung from the top was broken in half.

"Get the ladder under my feet! Hurry!" The old man's voice was strong, but he was breathing hard.

Nick and Chad tried to lift the ladder, but it was too big and old and heavy. So Addie and Emily got on one side and the boys got on the other. Together they managed to lift the ladder into the air. It was awkward and wobbling badly. After several tries, they were able to hold it steady directly under Frank Danner.

The old man found the top rung with his feet and used it for traction to push himself back into the hayloft.

The children held the ladder in place until they were sure Mr. Danner was safe on the floor of the loft. Then they let the ladder drop against the wall with a loud bang.

No one said anything for several long moments. Addie couldn't stand it. "Mr. Danner?" she called. "Are you okay?"

"Yes," he said shortly. "Let me rest."

They waited in silence. Finally they heard the old man clear his throat. "Would two of you hold the ladder? I'm going to try this again."

Though the ladder was leaning against the wall, Nick and Chad steadied it on both sides. Frank Danner made his way down, skipping the second rung and testing each rung gingerly before he put his full weight on it. Finally he was at the bottom, and everyone began breathing normally again.

The old gentlman took a handkerchief out of his pocket and wiped the sweat from his forehead. Then he glared at the four children. "What are you doing here?" he asked. "I thought I told you to stay off my property."

"You'd be dead if we weren't here!" Emily practically shouted.

"Emmie!" Chad hissed, and Emily frowned at him but she didn't say any more.

"What are you doing here?" Addie asked.

"It's my property," the old man said. "Why shouldn't I be here?"

"Did you find it?" Nick asked him.

Frank Danner frowned at the young boy. Then he began looking around the floor of the barn. "I dropped it when the ladder fell," he said.

Addie saw it first, and she ran to the corner of the barn where the oilskin package lay. It was bigger than the first three, and there was obviously more in this package than just a little wooden man. She handed the package to Mr. Danner, and he felt the contents carefully.

He was evidently disappointed because he shook his head and gave the package to Emily. "It's not what I'd hoped for," was all he said when Emily looked at him in surprise.

"But," Addie was confused, "what were you hoping for?"

Frank Danner smiled sadly. "I was hoping to find the scarlet box."

"Here It Begins, and Here It Ends..."

Addie took a deep breath before she spoke. "We have the scarlet box."

Mr. Danner stared at the young girl. So did Chad and Emmie.

"No, we don't," Emmie said.

"Yes, we do." Addie kept her eyes on Frank Danner. Even in the shadows of the barn, she could tell his face had lost some of its color.

"It was one of the things Sidney packed in the metal box we found in the creek."

"You never told us about it!" Emmie cried.

Nick shrugged. "I think we were all so interested

in the clues and the toys, we forgot about it. It didn't seem as interesting."

"Where is the box now?" Frank asked.

"It's at my house," Nick told him. "I think Mom put it back in the lockbox."

"May I see it?" the old man asked.

"Of course," Nick stammered. "It's yours."

"Let me give you a ride home," he said and nodded toward the last stall in the barn. "I can bring you back for your bikes later," he told Chad and Emily.

"You knew we were here?" Emily asked in amazement.

Frank Danner frowned. "Certainly. Why do you think I called for help? To hear myself talk?"

Nick chuckled under his breath, and the other children smiled. Frank Danner turned and left the barn.

The boys and Addie got to the car first, and Emily was stuck riding in the front seat with her great-uncle. Frank talked quietly as they made the short trip to Nick's house, and the children listened with great interest.

"Sid and I were always as different as night and day. When we got along we were the best of friends. When we didn't—" Frank just shook his head and didn't finish the sentence.

"I was always serious, Sid was a joker," he continued. "He loved games of any kind. You've probably figured that out by now. Scavenger hunts were one of his favorites. When our folks died and we had to take over the farm, I thought he'd change. But he didn't."

Frank smiled to himself. "It's probably just as well. I was serious enough for both of us. Then the war came and everything changed."

"Why didn't Sidney get—" Addie searched for the phrase Miss T. had used. "Why didn't Sidney get called up?"

"Sid had polio as a boy. Only a mild case, but it left him with a game leg. So Sid had to stay home and farm the land. Of course, I thought he'd fail miserably. And he was angry because I got the 'privilege' of going to war."

"So he went and married your girlfriend," Nick said.

Frank laughed for the first time, and it was a deep, throaty chuckle. "That was the biggest favor Sid ever did for me."

Emily glared at Frank, and he smiled at his niece. "I know she was your great-grandmother, but she wasn't my type. We fought about everything. So I introduced her to Sid. And of course, he married her.

"No," he continued, "Stella was not the source of our argument."

"What was?" Addie had to ask.

"The scarlet box," Frank answered.

He pulled into Nick's drive, and the children all piled out of the car. Nick led the way inside to the kitchen. The house was empty.

"Mom and Jess and Mrs. Tyler are out looking at the garden," Nick said after he'd checked the back-yard.

"Good." Frank hesitated. "I'm not quite ready to face Sarah yet," he said. "May I see the things you've found?"

Addie brought all the toys in from the laundry room while Nick opened the lockbox and removed the leather bag. They set everything on the kitchen table.

Emily still held the last oilskin bag. "We have to open this too," she said.

"Let's wait," Chad told her. "Until . . . Uncle Frank has seen everything else."

Addie removed the scarlet box from the leather bag and opened it. She unfolded the first piece of paper. "We found this letter and the first clue and these marbles in the scarlet box." She handed the letter to the elderly man. He read it quickly and glanced at the toys in front of him.

"Sid and I made those," he said. "Mama thought they were wonderful, so she saved them." He picked up the wooden horse. "This was my first attempt at carving." He turned the horse over in his hand and studied it for several moments. Then he set it down. "Where is the first clue?"

Addie handed him the paper, and he began to read out loud.

"'Here it begins and here it ends, always brothers, sometimes friends.'" Frank pressed his lips together and finished reading the clue in silence. "The loose bricks in the root cellar," he said in a rough voice when he was done.

Addie nodded and handed him the first little wooden man. Frank took the crude figure and smiled. "This was Sid's first attempt at carving," he said.

Nick gave him the second clue, and he read it silently. Then he looked at the children in amazement. "You found our secret slot under the bridge?" he asked.

Addie grinned. "It took us a while, but we found it."

Nick gave him the second wooden figure. "That's where this guy was hidden."

"Ah, Tom Sawyer," Frank murmured. "I carved this one. Of course, I had to make him fancier than Sid's, so I painted him."

Emily had the third clue and the cowboy, and she gave them both to her uncle eagerly. "This is the one we helped find," she said.

"Sid's cowboy," Frank said. He read the paper and began to smile. "But I thought Nellie was destroyed during the tornado!" he exclaimed.

Chad nodded. "The tornado took down the gazebo and the statue in Westside Park, but the park district stored Nellie in a shed until they could junk her. That's where we found her."

Frank was still shaking his head in puzzlement. "How did you figure this one out?" he wanted to know.

"Jerome Harris told us all about Nellie and the 'Star Spangled Banner,'" Emily said.

Frank chuckled out loud. "Then you know what happened to me." His chuckle faded to a sigh. "My only regret was that I never got to sing the song."

Nick grinned. "I sang it for you."

The old man patted Nick's arm awkwardly. "Thanks," was all he said.

"And you have the fourth clue," Chad reminded him.

Frank nodded. "'Hidden away, hot and high, where the flies buzz and the dust flies,'" he said. "We spent some long, lazy days playing in that hayloft, jumping out of it. Open the package."

Nick already had the scissors out, and Emily cut the package open with trembling hands. She pulled out the last wooden figure, and everyone shouted in delight.

This man was the most sophisticated of them all. He had slick black hair and a black mustache, with a cigar in his mouth. He wore a black suit with a white shirt and black tie. There was a white handkerchief painted in his front pocket, and his shoes were black with white tips.

"He looks like a gangster," Nick said.

"He is," Frank smiled. "That's Al Capone."

"There are some other things in here," Emily said, and she handed the bag to her uncle.

Inside the bag were two sturdy blocks of wood. Each block had a smaller, rectangular wooden post glued to one edge. There were also five small wooden balls, each with a hole through its center, two wooden end caps, and a long, quarter-inch dowel. Mr. Danner laid all the pieces on the table and began assembling them.

He slid one of the wooden balls down the length of the dowel. Then he took the first wooden man and inserted the dowel through the arm holes. A second wooden ball followed and then came Tom Sawyer. Another wooden ball followed Tom and next came the cowboy. The fourth wooden ball was added and Al Capone finished the line up. The fifth wooden ball came last.

Frank held the row of figures and nodded toward the table. "Set those bases up with the posts facing one another," he told Chad. Chad held the bases in place while Frank slipped each end of the dowel in a hole at the top of each post. He placed the wooden end caps over each end of the dowel and tapped them in place with the handle of the scissors.

Now the wooden figures hung suspended from the dowel, and they swung gently back and forth. Frank placed the whole thing at one end of the kitchen table. Then he took a marble from the scarlet box and rolled it towards the toy. The marble struck the white tips of Al Capone's shoes, and the gangster flipped end over end. Everyone cheered.

"This was our favorite toy," Frank said when everyone was quiet. "We played with it for hours. Sid knew how much this meant to me."

"It's a great toy," Emily agreed, "but what does it have to do with the scarlet box?"

The old man sighed. "Nothing—and everything."

The four children exchanged confused glances. Mr. Danner picked up the antique box and began his story.

"This box has been in our family for more than one hundred and thirty years. My great-grandfather brought it home from the Civil War. He was a Union general. He took this from a southern plantation, before he and his soldiers burned the plantation to the ground."

Emily looked dismayed and Frank shrugged. "It was war." He continued the story.

"My great-grandfather gave the box to my grandfather, who carried it through the Spanish-American war. My father carried it through World War I. It became a source of pride for our family—proof that we had defended our country and came home victorious.

"Sid was very bitter when he was turned down for active duty during World War II. He assumed I would take the box with me to Europe, but I refused."

"Why?" Chad asked.

"Because I hated war."

"But you fought anyway," Nick protested.

"Of course," Frank said. "But not simply to carry on a family tradition. I fought so that other children could grow up in peace, the way I did. Every kid should have the chance to play under a bridge, jump out of a hayloft—or play marbles all day long with his brother."

He reached into his shirt pocket and took out four flat wooden buttons, each with a hole in its center. "That's why I carried these with me instead."

One by one, he placed a button hat on each of the four wooden figures. Then he took all four marbles and rolled them in quick succession. One by one, the hats flipped off as the figures tumbled. Emily picked them up and put them back on the men.

They each took turns rolling the marbles. Nick did the best and got three hats off on the first try. Emily missed them all. Frank watched the children play, and Addie was sure she saw a little anger and bitterness fade from his expression every time a marble hit its mark.

Thank You, Lord, she prayed. *Thank You for letting me see this.*

"Mr. Danner," Addie asked, watching Chad roll the marbles, "don't you think your brother and your father and all your other relatives felt the same way you did?"

Frank Danner nodded slowly. "I do now. At the time, I thought they were full of pride. They glorified war, and there is nothing glorious about it. But it finally occurred to me that I grew up in peace because they risked their lives for me first. *That* was the real tradition they passed on." He ran one finger over the painting of the soldier on the lid of the scarlet box. "I was just too stubborn to try and understand what Sid was telling me."

"I think you should have taken the box *and* the buttons to Europe," Emily said. She dropped the four wooden hats inside the scarlet box and snapped the lid on. "Then you and Sid would both have been happy and never had that fight."

Frank took the box from his niece and smiled at the young girl's simple solution. "The perfect compromise," he agreed. "I never got the chance to tell Sid I was sorry, but I think he knew," he said, gesturing to the toys scattered on the table.

"I'm sure he did," Addie said quietly. She handed Mr. Danner a small slip of paper. "This was inside the last bag."

Frank took the paper and read it. A slow smile spread over his face, and he read the verse out loud.

Here it begins, and here it ends,
Always brothers, forever friends.
Disagreements fade, heartaches cease,
And a family's lasting love brings peace.

Don't Miss Any of the
Addie McCormick Adventures!
by Leanne Lucas

The Stranger in the Attic
A vanishing visitor and secrets from the past . . . Can Addie and Nick put the puzzle together before something terrible happens to their friend Miss T.?

The Mystery of the Missing Scrapbook
A missing scrapbook, mysterious paintings, and an old letter lead Nick, Addie, and Brian on a heartstopping chase. Are they in over their heads this time?

The Stolen Statue
A movie star has been kidnapped and Miss T.'s statue has disappeared! Addie has all the clues . . . but can she put them together before it's too late?

The Chicago Surprise
When Addie and Nick catch a thief, they discover more about the culprit than they bargained for!

The Mystery of the Skeleton Key
In Addie's family history, there's a "treasure" that no one can find! Will Addie be able to solve a mystery that's more than 100 years old?

The Computer Pirate
Someone is stealing information from the school's computer system! Addie's friend is the #1 suspect. Can she prove his innocence?

The Secret of the Scarlet Box
Addie and Nick find an old lockbox with clues for a special scavenger hunt. Can they find the treasure before anyone else?

The Action Never Stops in
The Crista Chronicles
by Mark Littleton

Secrets of Moonlight Mountain

When an unexpected blizzard traps Crista on Moonlight Mountain with a young couple in need of a doctor, Crista must brave the storm and the dark to get her physician father. Will she make it in time?

Winter Thunder

A sudden change in Crista's new friend, Jeff, and the odd circumstances surrounding Mrs. Oldham's broken windows all point to Jeff as the culprit in the recent cabin break-ins. What is Jeff trying to hide? Will Crista be able to prove his innocence?

Robbers on Rock Road

When the clues fall into place regarding the true identity of the cabin-wreckers, Crista and her friends find themselves facing terrible danger! Can they stop the robbers on Rock Road before someone gets hurt?

Escape of the Grizzly

A grizzly is on the loose on Moonlight Mountain! Who will find the bear first—the sheriff's posse or the circus workers? Crista knows there isn't much time—the bear has to be found quickly. But where, and how? Doing some fast thinking, Crista has a plan...

Danger on Midnight Trail

Crista can't stand her cousin Sarah, who does *everything* better. When an overnight hike into the mountains turns into a nightmare, can Crista and Sarah put aside their differences to save Crista's dad and face the danger on Midnight Trail?

Find Adventure and Excitement in
The Maggie's World Series
by Eric Wiggin

Maggie: Life at The Elms

Maggie's father died at the Battle of Gettysburg, and the man her mother is going to marry has a son who Maggie just can't stand! She asks for permission to live with her Grandpa at his special home, The Elms.

Little does Maggie know how much her life is about to change—all because of a sharp-tongued girl at a logging camp and surprising lessons about friendship and forgiveness.

Maggie's Homecoming

After two years in the deep woods with Grandpa, Maggie is eager to return home. She and her stepbrother, Jack, must learn to get along—and to everyone's amazement, they do!

One Saturday she and Jack decide to explore a long-abandoned farmhouse around the mountainside—only to find out the place isn't abandoned after all . . .

Maggie's Secret Longing (available January 1995)

Maggie's first job follows quickly after her graduation from high school. She's now "Miss Maggie"—the schoolmarm for a merry lot of country urchins with a bent toward creative mischief.

A surprise romance beckons at Maggie's heart as well, until a sudden series of events casts doubt about her future with the young, handsome Terry MacAlester.